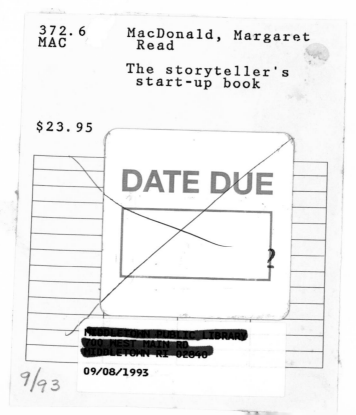

The Storyteller's
Start-Up Book

Also by
Margaret Read MacDonald

The Storyteller's Sourcebook: A Subject, Title, and Motif Index to Folklore Collections for Children

Twenty Tellable Tales: Audience Participation Folktales for the Beginning Storyteller

Booksharing: 101 Programs to Use with Preschoolers

When The Lights Go Out: Twenty Scary Tales to Tell

The Skit Book: 101 Skits from Kids

Look Back and See: Twenty Lively Tales for Gentle Tellers

The Folklore of World Holidays

Peace Tales: World Folktales to Talk About

Tom Thumb (Oryx Multicultural Folktale Series)

The Storyteller's
Start-Up Book

Finding, Learning, Performing, and
Using Folktales
Including Twelve Tellable Tales

Margaret Read MacDonald

Published 1993 by August House, Inc.,
P.O. Box 3223, Little Rock, Arkansas 72203,
501-372-5450.

Printed in the United States of America
10 9 8 7 6 5 4 3 2 1

LIBRARY OF CONGRESS
CATALOGING-IN-PUBLICATION DATA

MacDonald, Margaret Read, 1940-
The storyteller's start-up book : finding, learning, performing,
and using folktales including
twelve tellable tales / Margaret Read MacDonald
p.   cm.
Includes bibliographical references and index.
ISBN 0-87483-304-3 : $23.95
—ISBN 0-87483-305-1 (pbk.) : $13.95
1. Storytelling. 2. Storytellers—Training of.
3. Folklore. I. Title.
LB1042.M23   1993
372.64'2—dc20   93-1580

Executive editor: Liz Parkhurst
Assistant editors: Jan Diemer, Stephen Buel
Design director: Harvill Ross Studios Ltd.
Cover design: Bill Jennings
Typography: Heritage Publishing Co.

Thanks to these storytellers, who have given permission for
their ideas to be quoted here: Rives Collins and Pamela J.
Cooper; Rex Ellis; Gail De Vos; Debra Harris-Branham; Erica Helm
Meade; Spencer G. Shaw; Jimmy Neil Smith; and Diane Wolkstein.

This book is printed on archival-quality paper that meets the
guidelines for performance and durability of the Committee
on Production Guidelines for Book Longevity of the
Council on Library Resources.

AUGUST HOUSE, INC.   PUBLISHERS   LITTLE ROCK

*T*his work is dedicated to

the countless children's librarians and teachers

who understand that our children need

to hear and see the *finest* artistry

this world has to offer.

May you continue to speak out

against authors, artists, publishers,

and even storytellers who would offer

second-rate work that they call

"good enough for children."

CONTENTS

An Invitation to Storytell

If you have this book in your hands you must be curious to know more about the art of storytelling. Perhaps you have heard a storyteller and thought, *I wonder if* I *could do that?* Perhaps a colleague or teacher has suggested that you might enjoy telling stories to the children or adults with whom you work.

The Storyteller's Start-Up Book intends to convince you that preparing stories is easy and that telling them is such fun you will never want to stop once you have started.

Today hundreds of professional storytellers are circling the world sharing their tales. Do not be intimidated by their skill and polish. We need such artists to inspire us; but even more we need caring tellers in every home and community who will share story with the personal warmth and concern that only the intimacy of small-group storytelling can provide.

You are to become one of those sharing tellers.

I have prepared this book as a starting place for the beginning storyteller. I include techniques for learning and performing story and for designing a story event; criteria for the selection of storytelling material; many suggestions for settings in which you may use your storyteller's art; ideas for incorporating storytelling into the classroom; and ways to *play* with story in any setting. For each of these topics I provide selected bibliographies featuring the books I feel will most help you on your way. To help you keep your commitment to storytelling I provide information about networking with other tellers. Most importantly, I attempt to convince you, the would-be teller, that the telling of a story is a *gift*—a special joy which you can share.

To help get you started, I provide twelve lively, easy-to-learn tales that other beginners have enjoyed—a few for each listening level from preschool to teen. And hints and bibliographies are here to help you locate more tellable tales.

My notes on learning a tale are designed to help you learn a story without stress. I offer a list of books written by other storytelling instructors in case my approach doesn't fit your personal learning style.

I have also provided a litany of the reasons people need to hear story. Use this to convince your supervisor that what you're doing is indeed important, even though it sounds like you're having way too much fun to be *working*.

Know that there are as many storytelling styles as there are tellers. Once you have your footing as a teller, you will want to explore material beyond that which I can offer here. Bibliographies within this book suggest places to begin thinking about personal stories, myths, religious tales, and other genres. Keep listening, reading, and experiencing story until you find just the right mix for you and your audiences.

Storytelling offers many things to those who choose it. Stories can teach, nourish, inspire. They can carry a burden of political message, sometimes without breaking. It is clear that stories change to fit our worlds. Conversely, stories *may* change our worlds.

To this teller, story is joy, play. It is a chance to share this joy with story listeners. The story event can range from quiet, intense listening to group playfulness which erupts into song and dance. The key to successful telling lies in nurturing and caretaking the audience—communicating directly with each listener.

Everyone can join in this art of storytelling. Here is a gentle, homely art that can take a lifetime of apprenticeship and still yield new rewards at every turn. But this simple art is so accessible that you can hear just one small tale ... and begin tomorrow to *pass it on!*

Your Place in Tradition

Everyone has a story to tell. And while we could spend a lifetime learning the art and technique of storytelling—perfecting our style and performance— for most of us, it is the simple telling of a tale that's important. Something as ordinary as the events of the day, an old joke, or a traditional story we heard as a child. Storytelling comes from the heart, not the head, and nothing should keep us from the exhilaration and sheer pleasure of telling a story.

—Jimmy Neil Smith,
Homespun: Tales from America's Favorite Storytellers

Many tellers, many tellings: It is good for us to realize that each teller who receives a tale filters that story through his or her own being to produce yet another variation on a theme. No two tellers present their tales in exactly the same way. Each new teller brings another perspective, another way of telling to the tale. And *all* are useful.

Just as there are many telling *styles,* there is no *correct* version of a folktale. There are myriad retellings, each differing from the others. The version you find in print represents only one telling of one teller at one moment in time. It has been frozen by pen or recorder. Now it is your turn to thaw out that story and let it resume its natural course of change as it meanders on from teller to teller.

Here are descriptions of three storytellers. Their styles are very different, but all were effective. Do not be afraid to develop your own style of telling. First, a Norwegian tale teller in the late 1800s:

One cannot say he related his folktales, he played them: his whole person, from the top of his shoes, was eloquent; and when he came to the place in the story where Aske-ladd had won the princess and all was joy and wedding bells, he danced the "Snip! snap! snout! My tale is out!" to an old rustic measure.[1]

A description of Gypsy tellers in Hungary early in the twentieth century:

When the narrator was in a good mood, he acted out the tales more than he recited them. With the Kolderascha tribe it was the custom to tell stories during work, and often the plot of the tale was represented in drama form. "Sometimes there were four of us or even five who told tales. One was the wolf, the other a prince, the third was a giant, or caliph, or whoever was needed. This was real theater, do you understand? It could start in the midst of work. The others went on working, but in time when the action got more and more exciting, they did not care a bit for anything else and did nothing but listen, waiting their turn. For the farther the märchen progressed, the more people appeared. So, one, for instance, was to be the judge and immediately he sat down, his legs folded under him, twirled his moustache, and making a solemn face he started judging and talking wildly. And there was the accused standing before him, bowing deeply and full of fear. And there were the guards, and the people, and God knew what else!"[2]

A New Guinea teller shows a totally different manner:

> She approached the kinihera with her cus-
> tomary air of composure and self-posses-
> sion. In all the narratives she told she spoke
> quietly but confidently, without hesitating
> and without allowing action to substitute
> for words at especially dramatic moments.[3]

Lively, restrained, dramatic, or quiet, the world of story embraces all styles. This telling that we do is greeted in today's world with the excitement reserved for a new discovery. But its roots are as old as the human race. Surely those most ancient drawings that decorate our ancestors' caves must have been a visual record of story being told in that time. Some of the earliest recorded story texts left to us were imprinted on clay tablets by Middle Eastern societies nearly four thousand years ago. One Babylonian tale begins:

> After God had created heaven,
> heaven created earth,
> earth created rivers,
> rivers created ditches.
> ditches created mud,
> mud created the worm.[4]

Speak these words aloud. You are hearing the beginning of a four-thousand-year-old story. As you enter the realm of storytelling, stop for a moment to consider the antiquity of this tradition. You are about to take your place in a chain of tellers. The tales in this book did not spring from my own imagination. They came from the mouths of storytellers ... who heard them from tellers ... who heard them from tell-ers.... The chain stretches back and back, perhaps farther than we can understand.

Early in this century the Arctic explorer Knud Rasmussen collected Eskimo tales of heroes confronting creatures resembling mammoths. For how many centuries must these tales have endured, tales framed in the days when mammoths still roamed the northlands?

In Theodor Gaster's *Oldest Stories in the World,* Gaster

presents translations of Assyrian, Babylonian, Canaanite, and Hittite stories found on cuneiform tables. The oldest of these dates from around 1600 BC. Reading through this collection, I came upon an unfinished tale. "Here the tablet is broken," Gaster tells us. "And the story's ending is unknown."

But I had a good idea how that story would have ended. Just that week I had read in a collection of Russian folktales a very similar story ... with the ending intact. The tablet engraved nearly four thousand years ago had broken, but the oral tale had survived, passing from mouth to mouth through the centuries. There is something remarkable about a tradition with this tenacity. This *story* with which we dabble is powerful stuff. It will outlive us all.

It has been said, "The poet lights a candle, and then goes out." Each of you, with your stories, will light small candles. And who knows what flames take fire from your candle.

NOTES

[1] Knut Liestol, *The Origin of the Icelandic Family Sagas* (Cambridge, Massachusetts: Harvard University Press, 1930), 102.

[2] Linda Degh, *Folktales and Society* (Bloomington: Indiana University Press, 1969), 184.

[3] Catharine Berndt, "The Ghost Husband," in *The Anthropologist Looks at Myth,* by Melville Jacobs and John Greenway (Austin: Published for the American Folklore Society by the University of Texas Press, 1966), 244.

[4] Theodor H. Gaster, *The Oldest Stories in the World* (Boston: Beacon Press, 1952), 93.

BIBLIOGRAPHY

To understand more about the place of story in oral tradition, browse in these:

Chase, Richard. *Grandfather Tales.* Boston: Houghton Mifflin, 1948. See pages 1-17 and the conclusion of each chapter for a reconstruction of an evening of family storytelling among Chase's Appalachian informants.

Glassie, Henry. *Passing the Time in Ballymenone.* Philadelphia: University of Pennsylvania Press, 1982. No folktales here, but lots of pleasing talk and a chance to watch an insightful folklorist looking at culture.

MacDonald, Margaret Read. "Origins of the Folktale Text." In *Twenty Tellable Tales,* 192-97. New York: The H.W. Wilson Co., 1986. Notes on tale collecting and performance style.

Pellowski, Anne. *The World of Storytelling: A Practical Guide to the Origins, Development, and Applications of Storytelling.* Expanded and

Revised Edition. New York: The H.W. Wilson Co., 1990. Drawing on years of research, Pellowski discusses the history of storytelling, and pays particular attention to the many unusual forms in which story is presented around the world—bardic storytelling, storytelling with objects, story with musical accompaniment. Fascinating to browse through, with an extensive bibliography.

Toelken, Barre. *The Dynamics of Folklore.* Boston: Houghton Mifflin, 1979. An overview of many areas of folklore research. Read and dabble in this book to understand the way contemporary folklorists look at culture. Toelken's bibliographic notes will guide the serious student to a more in-depth study of folklore.

Wolkstein, Diane. *The Magic Orange Tree and Other Haitian Folktales.* New York: Schocken Books, 1980. In notes preceding each tale, Wolkstein tells us about each teller's performance and his or her audience's reaction. Read these notes to witness the variety of folktale performance within one culture.

Learning the Story
in One Hour

Here is something you can learn as you go along.
Apply everything that comes your way to a better
understanding and use of it. Be your own teacher and
your own critic, develop that love and propensity for
it that can bring such immeasurable returns. We can
give you a starting-point; go on from here with a stout
heart.

—Ruth Sawyer, *The Way of the Storyteller*

To begin, you will search for a story that delights you.
This tale will be so wonderful you can't *wait* to go tell it. The
chapter entitled "Finding the Story" on page 63 will help you
in this search for your perfect tale. But for now, let's assume
you have that story in your hand. Soon it will be in your *head!*

You have discovered your own special story and are
ready to learn it. Block one hour to work alone, and begin.

1. Select.

Start with a story that you are eager to learn. When you
finish reading a tale and jump up with excitement, exclaiming,
"I can't *wait* to tell this!"—*that's* the tale you want to learn.
Don't waste your time on material that doesn't inspire this
eagerness to tell. And it may take quite a search to find a
handful of these gems that feel just right for your telling.

2. Concentrate.

Isolate yourself from clamoring children, ringing phones, and other interruptions. Be prepared to pace, talk out loud, and gesticulate. Some learners work well sitting quietly, but many find the intense energy needed to internalize a story calls for a body on the move.

3. Vocalize.

Read your story out loud. You have already read it silently several times in the process of choosing it for telling. Now listen to the language as you read aloud. Highlight any phrases which seem especially lovely or memorable. You may want to keep these in your own telling. Note any chants, songs, or onomatopoetic words which need to be retained intact in your retelling. Are the story's opening and closing so culture-specific or so well-written that you want to reproduce them exactly?

4. Memorize Key Bits.

Memorize the chants, songs, and key phrases you have marked. Do not worry about getting songs exactly right. Songs change from singer to singer just as stories change from teller to teller. Try to use song in your tale in the same way your source used it—to carry the plot forward, or to amuse and engage your audience—but do not worry because you cannot reproduce the tune and rhythm of the musical notation. Unless you are a skilled ethnomusicologist, you are unlikely to come close to an accurate reproduction of another culture's music. The important thing is that the story be shared and that the *intent* of the story's music be communicated.

5. Analyze.

Note the tale's basic structure. Some teachers recommend writing an outline of the tale at this point. I find that unnecessary unless you rely heavily on visual cues in learning. Just *notice* the tale's structure. For example the structure of "Turtle of Koka" (given in full on p. 111) is quite simple:

Opening: Turtle is caught.

First Episode: Turtle is threatened with axe.

                           Turtle sings that axe cannot harm him.

Second Episode: Turtle is threatened with hammer.

                           Turtle sings that hammer cannot harm him.

More episodes follow the same pattern, as many as the teller wishes.

Ending: Turtle escapes.

An awareness of this simple story structure is about all you need to tell that particular tale. Others are more complicated, but having a sense of the tale's structure will help you find your way through the story should you become befuddled.

6. Say the Story.

Put down the book and begin telling the tale aloud. Tell it in your own words. If you forget, stop briefly to check your text, then continue or begin again.

7. Repair.

After you have told through the entire tale, recheck your marked text. Were there special phrases you had hoped to use which you omitted? Is there a spot where you muddle the action? Plan a path over any rough spots in your telling. Take time to retell aloud those bits that felt shaky.

8. Tell it Through.

Tell the tale once more. Try not to stop this time. Keep telling through to the end. Force yourself to improvise, and just keep telling. With practice you will gain confidence in your ability to ride over rough spots and keep the tale moving.

9. Evaluate.

Make a note of spots which still need improvement. Then congratulate yourself on the amazing progress you have already made with this tale. Imagine the fun you are going to have sharing this story with your audience.

A note on visualization: Many tellers believe it is important to take time to imagine visually each scene of the story. Some draw story maps or flow charts. If visual stimulation is important to your learning, take time to do this. The bibliography at the end of this chapter gives sources which will help you with visualization techniques. Some tellers learn entirely through oral and kinesthetic cues and do not use the visualization process in story learning. Try both, and decide which is best for you. Also notice that certain simple tales such as "The Gingerbread Boy" rely mainly on movement and sound and do not need much visualization, whereas a personal story of your childhood may need intense visualization before you can bring it to life for your audience.

Story Practice on the Go

The next step in your tale learning will occur as you go about your daily routine. Tell the tale out loud as you drive to work. Tell it in the shower. Take a brisk walk after lunch and tell the story to yourself as you stride along.

Find a few functional story-practicing slots in your day and use them whenever you have a new tale to learn. My own performance-day rehearsals are: Shower (first rehearsal); fifteen-minute commute to the library (second rehearsal); ten-minute break in staff-room courtyard (final rehearsal half an hour before storytime).

A Final Rehearsal

Plan a final rehearsal slot to take place just before you tell. This rehearsal should be high-energy, on your feet, an active telling. You want to awaken your body to its storytelling potential. You have to be ready to control and challenge your audience. This is your "stage warm-up." Tell the story aloud, facing your imaginary audience. Tell *to* them, communicating with them, as if they were really there.

Now all you have to do is go out there and tell it once more, this time to your audience. This time you will have their feedback to hold you up, so this telling will be the *easiest*.

Keep Telling

My theory of story learning is based on the premise that we learn by *doing*. Since storytelling is a group activity, it is difficult to perfect a tale without an audience. Learning a story alone in front of a mirror is rather like practicing dance steps without a partner. You can memorize the patterns, but the flow of the event cannot be learned until you engage with another. Rather than spend excruciating hours memorizing and rehearsing at home alone, I suggest you pick a great tale, learn its simple structure, play at putting it into your own words, and then begin *telling* it.

The trick is that you must tell it more than once. You must tell the tale several times, refining your telling with each experience. To do this, you must *arrange* storytelling opportunities. Tell the story to your own children at home, tell it to your class if you are a teacher, offer to share the story with your children's class if you are a parent, tell it at Sunday School, to your cub scout troop ...

And don't stop there. If you are a classroom teacher, ask another teacher to trade classes for fifteen minutes so you can tell to that class. Offer to tell to the kindergarten on your lunch break. Tell on campouts, at family picnics; gather the neighborhood children together and tell.

And remember that children will want to hear this story told *again*. You can tell the same story several times to one group, letting the children take on increasing ownership of the tale with each telling.

Keep Evaluating

After each telling, take time to evaluate. What went especially well? Did you add new elements to your telling which you would like to keep? Have bad habits crept in that you want to lose before the next telling? See page 28 for a self-evaluation form that you may find useful.

Save it for Later

After the tale has begun to take shape, tape one of your tellings. Simply slide a recorder unobtrusively under your chair and switch it on. Store the tape for future reference. When you want to tell this tale next year, you will not have to rely on your memory to recreate the tale. Simply play the tape and you will at once recall your own unique telling of the previous year. If you do not make this tape, it is probable that some of the delightful inventions which worked so well in this telling will be lost forever twelve months from now. It has happened to me; don't let it happen to you.

BIBLIOGRAPHY

Suggestions for Story Learning from Other Tellers

Breneman, Lucille N. and Bren Breneman. *Once Upon a Time: A Storytelling Handbook.* Chicago: Nelson-Hall Publishers, 1983.

Farrell, Catharine. *Storytelling: A Guide for Teachers.* New York: Scholastic Inc., 1991.

Livo, Norma J. and Sandra A. Rietz. *Storytelling: Process and Practice.* Littleton, Colorado: Libraries Unlimited Inc., 1986.

Sawyer, Ruth. *The Way of the Storyteller.* New York: Viking Press, 1942. Reprint c. 1962.

Schimmel, Nancy. *Just Enough to Make a Story.* Berkeley, California: Sisters' Choice Press, 1992.

Shedlock, Marie L. *The Art of the Story-Teller.* New York: Dover Publications Inc., 1951.

Visualizing Your Characters

Birch, Carol L. *Image-ination.* Frostfire, 1991. An audiocassette to lead you through an exploration of character and place.

Farrell, Catharine. *Storytelling: A Guide for Teachers,* 21-23. New York: Scholastic, Inc., 1991.

Ross, Ramon Royal. *Storyteller,* 45-46. Columbus: Merrill Publishing Co., 1980.

Performing the Story

You are prepared to tell your story, then forget yourself. You are the instrument; the story is the thing.

—Gudrun Thorne-Thomsen, *Storytelling and Stories I Tell*

You have learned a story. You have rehearsed it, imagining your audience. Now they are *there*. What do you do? You go to your audience with excitement, for you are about to give them such a delight—a *gift* you have for them. But in order to unwrap the gift you must first set the stage. You will not just plop this jewel down among the groceries on the kitchen cabinet. Instead, you will prepare a special place for it.

Set the Stage

Think carefully about your storytelling arena. You do not want distractions at your back—a door that could suddenly burst open, a clock the audience might watch, excessive visual clutter, or worse of all a grimacing child. Arrange your space to avoid such distractions. Ask the members of your audience to rearrange their seating if need be. Although you can tell stories effectively virtually anywhere, creating a special "story space" is useful. You might move the children to a rug in the corner of the classroom, or gather them in a corner of the playground with a fence or tree as a backdrop. When I told on the bookmobile in Hawaii my story space at one stop was limited to six beach mats thrown down in the middle of a tarmac parking lot. Of course, I preferred those stops where I could gather the children at the foot of a huge monkey-pod tree. But the mats served to define the story spot and helped us become a group.

- The story spot must define the event as something out of the ordinary.
- The story spot must help create group identity.
- The story spot must protect the group from distractions.

Prepare Your Audience to Listen

Do not begin your story until your listeners are settled into their listening positions. Make sure they are arranged so that you can maintain eye contact with each member of the group. Gently remove potential distractions, such as cats, balls, or squirt guns.

The Pregnant Pause

You have introduced your story. Your audience is ready. You are ready. In this moment you pause. Look your audience over, and *gather* them together as you prepare to begin.

The Opening Bridge into Story

You have carefully crafted your opening sentence for effect. You have delivered it with confidence. Your audience is skeptical, nervous; they are wondering if you can really do this.

It is *your* job to put them at ease. Convey your joy and your confidence in this story venture. You must literally *pick them up* with these first words and carry them confidently through the tale.

Your opening phrase is your bridge between the world of ordinary conversation and the other-world of story. This crossing must be both magical and deliberate.

Communicate

You are into the story—now all you have to do is *tell* it. This does not mean *recite* it, or *perform* it. This means *communicate* it. Speak *to* your audience. Look into their eyes, read their responses. Your thoughts should be on the communication with your audience ... not on your own appearance and performance flaws.

Pace Yourself

Be aware of the pacing of your tale at all times. Do not rush through it. Slow gently to a pause, then race into rapid-fire telling as the story suggests. Stop. Let the story fall to the ground like a drifting balloon. Then tap it into the air and begin again. Give your audience spaces to breath ... to contemplate within your story. Provide them rushes of activity and excitement. You will have planned all of this as you rehearsed. Now take the time to relax into your story and play with its pacing.

Caretake Your Audience

Throughout the telling stay in tune with your audience. You have carried them into this realm of story. They are *your* responsibility. Watch them, respond to them. Pace the story to fit their needs. Stretch to communicate with each listener.

Revel in Language

Lie back on your tale and revel in the beauty of its language. Take time to roll lush words around on your tongue. Give each gorgeous phrase its due. You are *performing* fine language, just as a musician performs a piece of music. Take care with your phrases and be confident in their potential for bringing joy to your audience.

Dance Your Story

Move your body with your story. Stand perfectly still, or move through your space as the story requires. Let the story tell you how to move.

Stay true to your own being, however. Do not attempt wild gestures if these feel unnatural to you. Develop your own style and take confidence in it. Two common mistakes made by tellers are (1) holding the body too rigid and not letting the story move the body naturally, and (2) gesticulating wildly and leaping about the room without control. Gestures are made potent by the *control* with which they are executed. Make a definite *end* to each movement. Give enough ... but not too much.

End with Confidence

The tale's ending is the bridge back from the other-world to the mundane. There must be a deliberate feeling of gently setting the audience back down into their own lives. They have journeyed with you and now the journey is done. The tale's end should have the sense of a goodbye kiss. Your final words must be well-rehearsed and delivered with care.

The Calm After the Tale

Rest quietly for a few moments after your tale's close. Let your listeners return at their own pace from the dream world of the story or recover in silence if this is one of those tales which ends in an exuberant rush.

Accept that You Have Performed Well and Pleased Your Audience

Learn to enjoy the pleasure of your audience. You have worked hard to perfect this tale. You have given pleasure. Let them give back to you through their laughter, their tears, their applause, and their words of appreciation.

Do not feel slighted, though, if your audience shows little response. Some tales do not evoke outward responses. Some audiences take tales in silence. It is often these very audiences which carry the tales home and cherish them. The tale received in silence may be the most powerful tale of all.

All this must sound intimidating. But my last advice is the most important of all:

Don't Worry about Performance Technique ... Just Tell!

Each of you has a teller inside ... a voice eager to share those tales it loves. Just relax. Embrace your audience, and let that teller out. Begin by sharing the tales you love most in a simple, direct way. Learn to love the rapport with your audience, the feel of words flowing across your tongue, that sense of images pouring from your heart into theirs. First experience the *joy* of telling ... then you will return to your tales with the desire to perfect them.

I refuse to even *discuss* technique with my students until they have had experience in shaping a tale through repeated tellings. I demonstrate for students a few simple, sure-fire tales, then ask them to pick one of those tales and pass it on to as many audiences as possible before the class meets again. No technique, no advice to remember, no way to do it right, no way to do it wrong. Just *tell.*

Storytelling is like swimming. No amount of advice you read or hear can help much until you have felt the buoyancy of the water. Once you have thrown yourself onto the waves and felt them push back, you can relax and take joy in that support.

So it is with storytelling. Once you have thrown yourself onto the audience and let them push back at your tale, you can let go of your fears and begin to play.

Remember not to take yourself too seriously. Just relax and enjoy sharing a good story. Later, if you want to perfect your tale as an *art form,* consult the sources in this chapter's bibliography. A high degree of artistry is not necessary or perhaps even useful for those of us who are not aiming at a career as a professional storyteller. We are about *joy,* not *art.* Your own unrehearsed telling may already be perfect for your needs. The rigors and terrors of polishing technique sometimes frighten tellers and cut off their creativity before they have had a chance to learn to love their own inimitable story style.

Tellers who love their tales and their audience almost always bring delight. Each of us is different—quietly seated or loudly leaping, speaking in cultured tones, or irreverently robust—and brings a unique perspective to the tale. No one else can tell the tale as you can tell it. Be proud of your gift to the tale. Rest assured that no matter how many famous tellers may take the stage, none of them can tell that tale quite the way *you* can.

Evaluating Your Performance

Here are some questions to help you think about your performance. As you answer them, consider also: What was the value of this performance to your audience? To you? To your group?

Communication and Audience Caretaking

- Did you really *see* your audience?
- Were you trying to communicate with them as you told?
- Were you caring for the audience and aware of their needs and responses?

Delivery

- Did you take time to pause and collect yourself and your audience before you launched into your tale?
- Was your ending skillful? Effective?
- Did you allow your listeners to savor the ending in their own ways before breaking the story trance?
- Did you use your voice well to carry your tale's meanings?
- Did your body tell the tale with you? If not, how can you help your body join your voice, mind, and heart in communicating with your audience?

Scripting

- Did the script communicate the tale's meanings well?
- Did the language flow easily?
- Was the language you spoke as fine as you had intended?
- Mark the text for spots you need to work on.

Control

- Were you in complete control of your story?
- Did you know what you wanted to communicate well enough to relax and enjoy the sharing?

To be able to answer yes to these questions you need only one thing—experience.

- Where can you tell this story again?

BIBLIOGRAPHY

Stage Fright

Ristad, Eloise. "Clammy Hands and Shaky Knees." In *A Soprano on Her Head,* 157-171. Moab, Utah: Real People Press, 1982.

Developing Characterization

Breneman, Lucille N. and Bren Breneman. "Working for Characterization" and "Working for Visualization." In *Once Upon a Time: A Storytelling Handbook*, 43-60 and 61-72. Chicago: Nelson Hall Publishers, 1983.

Delivery

Cassady, Marsh. "Delivering Your Story." In *Storytelling Step by Step*, 134-46. San Jose: Resource Publications, 1990.

Cooper, Pamela J. and Rives Collins. "The Stories in the Telling: Finding Your Own Voice." In *Look What Happened to Frog: Storytelling in Education*. Scottsdale, Arizona: Gorsuch Scarisbrick Publishers, 1992.

Sawyer, Ruth. "A Technique to Abolish Technique." In *The Way of the Storyteller*, 131-48. New York: Viking Press, 1962.

Schimmel, Nancy. "Telling a Story." In *Just Enough to Make a Story*, 9-13. Berkeley, California: Sisters' Choice Press, 1992.

Eye Contact

Breneman, Lucile N. and Bren Breneman. *Once Upon a Time: A Storytelling Handbook*, 70-71. Chicago: Nelson-Hall Publishers, 1983.

Body Language

Breneman, Lucille N. and Bren Breneman. "Working for Bodily Action and Control." In *Once Upon a Time: A Storytelling Handbook*, 75-85. Chicago: Nelson-Hall Publishers, 1983.

Livo, Norma J. and Sandra A. Rietz. "Learning Movement." In *Storytelling Activities*, 55-62. Littleton, Colorado: Libraries Unlimited, 1987.

Thinking of Story
as an Event

That evening Justine told "The Singing Bone" ....
The moon was full, the frogs croaking, the children
loud and noisy. A spark was running from storyteller
to storyteller ....

Yet despite the full support the audience gave
Justine during her story, when she came to the moral, a
man shouted, "It is not for you to draw those morals."
Justine was under twenty, outspoken and independent
in her ways. She would not be silenced. She shouted
back at him: "I have as much right as you!" ...

But before the argument could get underway,
another storyteller cried, "Cric?" and there were
sufficient cracs *for the story to begin. Story after story,*
I was learning. A story begins much before its
beginning.

—Diane Wolkstein,
The Magic Orange Tree and Other Haitian Folktales

The folklorist today looks at traditional tellers with an eye
to their *use* of story. The tale itself is only one part of the story
event. The interplay between audience and teller, the performance aspects of the telling, the context into which the tale is
played, the hidden agendas behind the telling, the way that
tale and that telling function within that society—all these are
of interest to the folktale scholar. We would do well to think

of these matters when planning and executing our own *story events.*

Plan the Effect You Wish to Have on Your Audience.

You will select your stories to please your audience, but perhaps also to *affect* them. If you have a hidden agenda behind your telling, be clear in your own mind about it and use your stories to their best effect. When telling to junior high audiences, I often tell "Owl" from Diane Wolkstein's *The Magic Orange Tree.* I do this because I want the boys in the group to know that, like owl, they may think themselves homely when in fact a girl may one day find them "striking." Being aware of this purpose to the telling, I take my time with the tale, I allow a great deal of silliness in playing it out, but as I approach the serious ending I make certain that my audience has calmed down and is receptive to the tale's strong message. Without this clear sense of purpose, I might muff the tale's final moment.

Control the Physical Space and Set Up the Magical Moment.

When planning your story event, consider the physical requirements of your program. Will you stand, sit, move about? A combination of all three? How will your listeners be arranged? In a semi-circle, in rows, or jumbled about on, under, and over the furniture? Will they be sitting on the floor, on chairs, on bleachers, in their beds? How crowded will they be?

In the previous chapter, we talked about the importance of choosing the story spot carefully. You can create an other-worldly aura in the story space with simple props such as a rug and story chair, a wall hanging, a plant, and an arrangement of books. The warm light of a floor or table lamp can enhance the story area, or you can use a magical "story candle." The candle's lighting signals entrance into the story realm; at story's end, it is extinguished with a wish. Professor Spencer Shaw uses entrancing rhymes to carry the audience over into story as he lights the story candle. Other tellers ring bells, open story bags, don story aprons—anything that sets the moment and the space apart. Of course your *attitude* in creating this story environment is most important of all. If *you* think of this moment as unique, it will become a point of entry into the world of story.

Plan a Flow for Your Program.

In planning a tale event, you must think of the programmatic aspects of the entire scene. Are you the only teller? Or do you share the time with someone else? Do you tell for an hour? Half an hour? If you will be telling more than one story, you need to think about the flow of the entire program.

What do you want to present in your first contact with the audience? You will need to interest them and convince them that time with you is going to be well spent. Your introductory comments and first story must meet the audience on *their* ground. Later in your program, after the audience has come to trust you, you can introduce material that they might not accept from a "stranger." In a school assembly, for example, I begin with an active, humorous tale. Having captured the students' attention and pleased my audience, I can later move on to quiet, more thoughtful pieces. Conversely, when telling to adults I may start with more sedate material and move into a playful audience participation tale only after I have won them over.

Consider the sequence in which you will tell your stories. If you tell four hyperactive audience participation stories in a row your listeners may be hanging from the ceiling ... or stretched out exhausted on the bleachers by the end of the last story. Pace your program, just as you pace your story. Add a calming tale into an active program. Or use an active tale to energize an audience during a quieter story session. Add poetry, music, and storytime stretches to rest your audience between tales. Listening is hard work. A break between tales is welcome and useful in lengthening the listening span of your audience.

Give careful thought to your program's ending. You will want to end on that emotional note you wish your listeners to carry away. Whether you end on a high or a low note is up to you. But the last tale's ending should be memorable.

Visualize Disaster ... and Avoid It!

Think ahead to envision both your audience and the setting. Control those factors you *can* control, and learn to live with those you cannot change. But thinking ahead prepares you for those unusual environments in which you may find yourself telling. If you agree to tell to children at a Christmas party, for example, assume that *unless you exert control over the situation* the smiling parents will plop two-year-olds in front of you and retreat to the punch bowl to chat with friends. Assume that each child will bear a sticky piece of candy cane. Assume that if a bell should happen to jingle, the children will all leap up and run toward the sound, abandoning you for Santa Claus. Think ahead and control anything you *can* to make your telling more successful.

Tailor Your Repertoire for Success in Varied Settings.

Knowing the composition of your audience in advance allows you to tailor your program to their interests and listening capabilities. The larger your repertoire, the easier it will be for you to plan programs that fit any eventuality.

In your repertoire, you will eventually need:

- two or three audience participation tales (those in this book will work) that will hold *any* audience, from preschool to adult;
- two or three challenging, meaningful pieces with content strong enough to interest and move an adult audience;
- two or three storytime stretches—songs or activities that get your audience up and stretching between stories;
- and one strong story which you love so much you can tell it anytime, anywhere, anyhow.

The latter is the one you trot out on the morning you wake up feeling bilious but just have to get through the story-time ... or the day Johnny brings his pet boa to class and insists on wearing it while you tell. In other words, you need one story you know well enough to tell on autopilot if need be. I don't recommend that you do that, but you need that story in your repertoire ... just in case.

BIBLIOGRAPHY

Establishing Storytelling Rituals

Livo, Norma J. and Sandra A. Rietz. "Bringing the Author In." In *Story-telling: Process and Practice*, 155-203. Littleton, Colorado: Libraries Unlimited Inc., 1986.

——————————. "Monitoring Pre-telling Protocols." In *Storytelling Activities*, 48-50. Littleton, Colorado: Libraries Unlimited, 1987.

Shaw, Spencer G. "Arrangement of Program Content" in "First Steps: Storytime with Young Listeners." In *Start Early for an Early Start: You and the Young Child*, edited by Ferne Johnson, 50-51. Chicago: American Library Association, 1976.

Storytime Songs, Games, and Stretches

These sources suggest songs, poems, games, and short audience partic-ipation tales to wake the audience up and give them a stretch.

Baltuck, Naomi. *Crazy Jibberish and Other Story Hour Stretches.* Hamden, Connecticut: Linnet Books, 1993.

Tashjian, Virginia. *Juba This and Juba That: Story Hour Stretches for Large and Small Groups.* Boston: Little, Brown & Co., 1969.

——————————. *With a Deep Sea Smile: Story Hour Stretches for Large and Small Groups.* Boston: Little, Brown & Co., 1974.

Fingerplays and Action Rhymes for Younger Listeners

Defty, Jeff. *Creative Fingerplays & Action Rhymes: An Index and Guide to Their Use.* Phoenix: The Oryx Press, 1992.

Playing with Story

*The attention of the group plays like a wind on the
storyteller's instrument. He tunes it and sets the key to
fit the particular group in front of him; he adjusts his
material to the composite listening ear of his group.
No two groups are alike nor is the same group in like
mood twice running. The art of the storyteller is the
most fluid of all the arts.*

—C. Madeleine Dixon, "Once Upon A Time," in *Storytelling*

I think of my own storytellings as group play. Together the
audience and I carry on this dance called story. Only *I* know the
steps, but their responses dictate the direction, speed, and
enthusiasm of our movement. At the heart of this approach is a
relaxed and joyful sense of entering into story-play together. I
am not performing *before* a group, I am sharing *with* them.

Playing with Story Through Audience Participation

All of the stories in this book will lend themselve to this
type of relaxed "playing with story." The audience will catch
on quickly to their "part." As you become more at-ease working with audiences, you can give the audience increasing free-
dom. Sometimes I engage in banter with audience members,
sometimes I pretend a child in the audience is a character from
my tale and initiate dialogue with that person. These improvi-
sations are not necessary to effective storytelling—and could in
fact hamper it if you don't keep a strong hand on your audience
and a keen sense of direction to your story—but this kind of
story-play can be a warm group-building device.

All of the stories in this book allow for audience participation through chants or songs. Some tellers like to rehearse their

song with the audience before the story begins so that they are ready to chime in when their part arises within the story. I usually just wait until the song makes its appearance in the tale. After I have sung it once by myself, I invite the audience, "Come on and help me with that song"; we all sing it again a time or two, and then the story progresses. Most audiences quickly pick up on the play between teller and audience in this type of storytelling. Usually a nod of your head and an encouraging glance are all that is needed to cue them to chime in. If they don't catch on at first, you can cue them with a question: "What did turtle say?" ("Turtle of Koka ...")

Occasionally you will encounter an audience that *will not* respond. If they clearly feel uncomfortable with this type of activity, just tell the story without their participation. One spring, while visiting schools to tout our summer reading club, I told Diane Wolkstein's "Uncle Bouki Dances the Kokioko" to two fifth-grade classes. The first class had a teacher who read to them, told stories to them, and played with them all year. They *and their teacher* were dancing in the aisles along with Uncle Bouki and myself. I bounced into the classroom next door ready to play Uncle Bouki all over again. Those students had a stiff teacher; no one spoke in that classroom without raising a hand, everyone sat upright at his desk at all times. *No one* would clap or sing along with me in that classroom. I didn't dare even *ask* them to get up and *dance.* We must adapt our methods to our audiences.

The second pitfall of audience-participation telling is the overly exuberant audience which gets so keyed up you lose control over them. A most horrifying example of that occurred when Jeff Defty, then a student librarian, and I were team-telling in an elementary school library. Jeff had just told a wonderful story about cats to two classes of kindergarteners sitting on the floor. He had the children *being* cats with him as he told the tale. He ended the tale with a flourish and dashed off in the same breath, "Now! Back to your classrooms!" The entire group swirled around and *crawled meowing* in a rushing mass out the library door and down the hall! They were half-way out the door before we recovered from our amazement and rushed to head them off.

Plan a way to bring your audiences down to a calmer level of reality before releasing them back into their own lives.

A student once complained that she had tried telling "Jack and the Robbers" and had been unable to stop the children once they started barking, meowing, crowing, and bellowing in response to the animals in the story. If your story calls for a loud cacophony of sound, be sure you are clear in your mind exactly how you will *start* the audience response ... and exactly how you will *stop* the audience response.

Plan a way to stop every audience response that you start.

Playing with Story Through Repeated Tellings

Any good story deserves more than one telling. Audiences love to hear these repeated. They will demand to hear some tales again and again. If an audience keeps demanding a story, keep telling it. This story may be meeting some need of the group which neither you nor they can define.

On repeated tellings the audience may take increasing control over the story. They may insist that it be told exactly the way they remember it, or they may begin suggesting ways to change the story. Stories with audience-participation opportunities are usually taken over with a fervor on repeated tellings. Soon the audience knows the entire tale from front to back. Their ownership of the tale becomes complete as they begin retelling the tale themselves.

Playing with Story Through Dramatic Play

On repeated tellings children soon show signs of wanting to "play" the story. They can barely sit still. They want to jump up and *be* the bears. Let them. You simply retell the story as they improvise its actions.

At first, younger children will throw their bodies into the

story more readily than their voices. Older children will prefer to improvise their own speaking parts. As teller, you provide "And the old bear said ..." and let the bear take it from there.

This is not "putting on a play"; this is simply "acting out a story." We are merely retelling with our bodies the story we have already loved through words. Let the story dictate your method here. With a two-character story such as "The Gunni-wolf," we can all act out both parts, changing from character to character as the dialogue progresses. Or we can divide the group into two camps, little girls and Gunniwolves, letting each side act one part. For tales with more characters, assign parts, letting several children perform each role together if necessary. Just be sure everyone gets to play.

Children find this dramatic play so rewarding that they will soon demand to act out *every* story you tell. This may not fit into your own plans. Select those stories you wish to move into dramatic play with care, and make it clear to the group that you will not "play" every story you share.

Playing with Story Through Music

As you begin playing with story, music may enter your tellings. Try retelling the story through song and rhythm.

Create songs or musical interludes to add into your story. Let the children help you. Create a poetic line—then just sing it. Sing it again another way. Choose the musical mood that best suits it and add another line to it. Let your audience play with it, expand it, change it.

Sing the entire story as an opera. Three eighth-grade boys in my class were shy about telling. They decided to *sing* "Henny Penny" instead. They simply began singing their parts to each other and soon had composed a delightfully rousing rendition. It was never written down, but it delighted the preschoolers for whom they performed.

Pass out rhythm instruments or discover found objects to make music on and create background music to accompany the tale's telling. Experiment. Shake, bang, and blow on everything in sight. Select your "instruments" and begin. Let the chorus improvise with their voices and instruments as you tell. Try retelling the entire story *without words,* using only sound and music.

Robert Barton and David Booth, in an article entitled "Feeling Like an Onion," tell of an ethereal telling of Joseph Jacob's "The Buried Moon," performed entirely in found sound. Anything the student could find to create sound was incorporated.

Playing with Story Through Movement

The introduction of music to your story will soon lead to movement. Add dance interludes to the story. Or portray the entire story through dance or mime. New Zealand teller Rangimoana Taylor tells each story twice—first in words, using much body language. Then he repeats the story using only dance. The result is entrancing.

Playing with Story Through Art

You can extend the story experience by allowing the group to draw images from the tale. Or devise an art project to carry on the theme of your story. After hearing a set of folktales about rice, my students drew scenes from the tales, gluing on rice grains as a design element. Creating masks or costumes to retell the story as drama can provide an exciting artistic extension of the story event.

Playing with Story Through Creative Writing

Let your children extend the story by writing their own alternative endings; writing of what happened *after* the story's ending; creating a diary which one of the characters might have kept during the story; or imagining their own story inspired by this one.

The Tale Stands Alone

Though it is fun to extend the story through drama, art, creative writing, music, and movement, remember that the *tale* stands alone. It needs no follow-up. Story is an end in itself.

BIBLIOGRAPHY

Audience Participation

MacDonald, Margaret Read. *Twenty Tellable Tales: Audience Participation Folktales for the Beginning Storyteller.* New York: The H.W. Wilson Co., 1986.

_____. *Look Back and See: Twenty Lively Tales for Gentle Tellers.* New York: The H.W. Wilson Co., 1991.

Miller, Teresa. *Joining In: An Anthology of Audience Participation Stories and How to Tell Them,* edited by Norma Livo. Compiled by Teresa Miller with assistance from Anne Pellowski. Cambridge, Massachusetts: Yellow Moon Press, 1988.

Tashjian, Virginia. *Juba This and Juba That: Story Hour Stretches for Large and Small Groups.* Boston: Little, Brown & Co., 1969.

_____. *With a Deep Sea Smile: Story Hour Stretches for Large and Small Groups.* Boston: Little, Brown & Co., 1974.

Creative Dramatics

Mason, Harriet and Larry Watson. *Every One a Storyteller: Integrating Storytelling into the Curriculum.* Portland, Oregon: Lariat Productions, 1991.

Sierra, Judy and Robert Kaminski. *Twice Upon a Time: Stories to Tell, Retell, Act Out, and Write About.* New York: The H.W. Wilson Co., 1989.

Incorporating Other Mediums

Barton, Robert. "Uncrating the Story: Storytelling in the Classroom." In *Tell Me Another: Storytelling and Reading Aloud at Home, at School, and in the Community*, 90-145. Markham, Ontario: Pembroke Publishing Ltd., 1986.

Herman, Gail N. *Storytelling: A Triad in the Arts.* Mansfield Center, Connecticut: Creative Learning Press, 1986.

Livo, Norma J. and Sandra A. Reitz. "Nonstory Resources." In *Storytelling: Process and Practice*, chapter 6. Littleton, Colorado: Libraries Unlimited, 1986.

Ross, Ramon Royal. "Choral Reading" and "Singing and Dancing." In *Storyteller*, 85-106 and 107-198. Columbus: Merrill Publishing Co., 1980.

Telling the Story with Music and Sound

Barton, Robert and David Booth. "Feeling Like an Onion." In *Writers, Critics, and Children.* New York: Agathon Press, 1976.

Teaching with Story

"I have learned," said the Philosopher, "that the head does not hear anything until the heart has listened, and that what the heart knows today the head will understand tomorrow."

—James Stephens, *Crock of Gold*

Justifying Story in the Curriculum

It always amazes me when teachers insist they have no time to fit storytelling into their curriculum. Most stories take less than ten minutes to tell. And stories can fit easily into many areas of the curriculum. Use nature tales to enhance science. Select tales from the cultures in your social studies units. Use singing tales in the music class. Match math puzzle tales to the math curriculum. And use *any* tale to enhance language arts. For specific ideas on matching storytelling activities to student learning objectives see the sources mentioned in the bibliography for this chapter.

Storytelling teaches listening. It models fine use of oral language. It models plot, sequencing, characterization, the many literary devices you wish to convey. There is no better educational tool to teach language-arts skills.

And yet teachers say, "If we get through our workbook, *maybe* we'll have time for a story." Teachers, the workbook will be forgotten by tomorrow, but the sound, the feel, the sense, the heart of that story may stay with the child as long as he lives. Make space in the classroom for true *quality* time today. Share a story.

The folktale has so much to teach us. It brings us the voice of the past and the voices of distant peoples. The tale speaks with human wisdom, it bounces into the lives of our children carrying the joy of another age, another people. Or it slides into our hearts bearing their sorrows, their wonderings. It should be received as tales have always been, as a simple gift dropped from one mouth to another. Let the children retell the tales orally, spoken again as they were in the past. Let the students play with the stories, acting them out, drawing them, dancing them, singing them. Use the folktale as a springboard into the worlds of cultures distant and past. Talk of the story and assess the humaneness of its actions. Wonder about its motives, its mysteries, its madness. Does the tale speak the truth?

Use tales also to lead students into the glorious worlds of literature and book illustration. Share beautifully illustrated editions of your tale; share literary pieces drawing on themes related to your story.

Many books have been written for the teacher suggesting story as a device for teaching structure, plot, characterization, and a plethora of other concepts. Story is suggested as a springboard for writing exercises. For many of these educators, the end toward which they move is the piece of student writing. The child hears a folktale told or read, dissects it via a chart, and finally writes a retelling or creates a new story copying that tale's form. If you *must* dissect the tale to meet your curriculum's guidelines, please commit this brutality only *after* everyone has had a good time, playing with their birthright—the untrammeled folktale.

A Sample Whole Language Web

The possibilities for whole language units built around story are endless. On p. 45 is a web prepared by three Seattle teachers using the story "Gecko" as its starting point.

Folktale Comparative Study

With older students you might want to continue your use of story with a comparative folktale study. The cross-cultural comparison of folktale variants provides an interesting multi-cultural activity. Take one tale—Cinderella for example—and share variants of this story from several cultures. Compare the story's elements to see which remain constant through various

SOCIAL AWARENESS
Feminist discussion: should a girl be a prize?
Acknowledgment of the debt society owes to the past:
Gecko succeeded by building on the digging efforts of the others.
Scientific discoveries are likewise possible only because of the
discoveries of those who have gone before.
Discussion of group heckling and individual feelings:
Awareness of Gecko's feeling when the others mocked him.
Gecko's refusal to give up: When is this a good quality?

SCIENCE
Drought
Ground water
Wells
Geckos, salamanders, lizards

SOCIAL STUDIES
Limba culture
West Africa
World view of drought-prone areas

GECKO
The animals compete at digging for water during a drought. A woman has offered her daughter as prize for the winner. Gecko continues to dig long after the others have given up. Tiny gecko wins.

MATH
Sorting by size
Size relationships

DANCE
Dance the
entire story.
Create dances to use
within the story...
a digging dance,
for example.

ART
Illustrate the tale
Cut sillouettes for the
tale's characters.
Create a diorama
Create masks to
act out the tale.

PHYSICAL ACTIVITY
Plan a stomping contest.

MUSIC
Retell the story by
singing it, opera style.
Accompany the story's telling with
musical instruments, with found
objects, or body music (hand claps,
leg slaps, humming, etc.)

DRAMA
Play the story as creative drama.
Perform the story as a play for others.
Perform the story as a masked play.
Perform the story as a puppet play.
Work on character development
for elephant, hippo, gecko,
and the others.

LANGUAGE ARTS
Read other stories from this culture.
Read other stories about drought situations.
Write a story inspired by Gecko. About another drought?
Another adventure of Gecko?
Write character sketches for elephant, hippo, gecko.
Create another expandable story like "Gecko"
in which you keep adding characters.
Use "Gecko" to talk about sequencing, rhythm,
other literary devices.

tellings and which change to adapt to the culture telling the tale.

To locate several versions of one tale use *The Storyteller's Sourcebook: A Subject, Title, and Motif Index to Folklore Collections for Children* by Margaret Read MacDonald (Neal-Schuman / Gale Research, 1982). See also *World Folktales: The Scribner's Resource Collection* by Atelia Clarkson & Gilbert B. Cross (Charles Scribner's Sons, 1980), which gives one version of several well-known tales and cites sources for variants. Titles in the Oryx Multicultural Folktales Series, which each provides around twenty-five versions of a well-known folktale, could also be useful (pp. 47-48).

Collecting Folklore

If you want to start a folklore-collecting project in your class, read *A Celebration of American Family Folklore: Tales and Traditions from the Smithsonian Collection* by Steven J. Zeitlin, Amy J. Kotkin, and Holly Cutting Baker (Pantheon Books, 1982). Working with tape recorders, notepads, or their memories, students can discover children's stories, family stories, family rhymes, riddles, sayings, and other genres of folklore.

My students brought in family heirlooms and wrote the stories they had been told about those pieces. The stories then were attached to the objects for future generations to discover. The students retold their family stories to the class. We selected our favorites to act out for parents in a special sharing in which we displayed heirlooms, photos, and family trees and told or dramatized the family stories. See this chapter's bibliography for sources that may help you start this sort of unit.

Begin sharing stories with the students in your classroom *now*.

Select ideas from this chapter and from the preceding chapter, "Playing with Story." Write a use for story into your lesson plans *today*. Or simply set aside fifteen minutes at the end of one day next week, gather the children around you, and tell your first story. It is really that simple. But you must *begin*.

BIBLIOGRAPHY

See the bibliography for "Teaching Others to Tell" (p. 52) for sources useful in teaching children to tell stories. See the bibliography for "Playing with Story" (p. 42) for ways to extend the story through creative dramatics, music and dance, and audience participation.

Barton, Robert. *Tell Me Another: Storytelling and Reading Aloud at Home, at School, and in the Community.* Markham, Ontario: Pembroke Publishing Ltd., 1986.

Barton, Robert and David Booth. *Stories in the Classroom: Storytelling, Reading Aloud and Roleplaying with Children.* Portsmouth, New Hampshire: Heinemann Educational Books Inc., 1990.

Blatt, Gloria T., ed. *Once Upon A Folktale: Capturing the Folktale Process with Children.* New York: Teacher's College Press, 1973. Articles by several authors suggesting classroom applications of the folktale.

Cooper, Pamela J. and Rives Collins. *Look What Happened to Frog: Storytelling in Education.* Scottsdale, Arizona: Gorsuch Scarisbrick Publishers, 1992.

De Vos, Gail. "Extensions for the Classroom." In *Storytelling for Young Adults: Techniques and Treasury*, 15-29. Littleton, Colorado: Libraries Unlimited, 1991.

Farrell, Catharine. "Stories to Tell: Story Plans and Classroom Activities, K-6." In *Storytelling: A Guide for Teachers*, 55-93. New York: Scholastic, Inc., 1991.

Hearne, Betsy. *Oryx Multicultural Folktale Series: Beauties and Beasties.* Phoenix: The Oryx Press, 1993.

Livo, Norma J. and Sandra A. Rietz. *Storytelling Activities.* Littleton, Colorado: Libraries Unlimited, 1987. Lots of great ideas for story-related activities.

——————————. "Storytelling at Home and School." In *Storytelling: Process and Practice*, 339-79. Littleton, Colorado: Libraries Unlimited, 1986.

MacDonald, Margaret Read. *Oryx Multicultural Folktale Series: Tom Thumb.* Phoenix: The Oryx Press, 1993.

Rosen, Betty. *And None of It Was Nonsense: The Power of Storytelling in School.* Portsmouth, New Hampshire: Heinemann Educational Books Inc., 1988. Thought-provoking commentary by a British teacher on her use of story with twelve- to sixteen-year old boys in a multicultural, inner-city school in Tottenham, England. She tells (folktale, myths, poetry) and elicits story (told and written, personal and imaginative) from her students.

Shannon, George. *Oryx Multicultural Folktale Series: A Knock at the Door.* Phoenix: The Oryx Press, 1992.

Sierra, Judy. *Oryx Multicultural Folktale Series: Cinderella*. Phoenix: The Oryx Press, 1992.

Developing a Unit for Cross-Cultural Study

Clarkson, Atelia and Gilbert B. Cross. *World Folktales: A Scribner Resource Collection*. New York: Charles Scribner's Sons, 1980.

MacDonald, Margaret Read. *The Storyteller's Sourcebook: A Subject, Title, and Motif-Index to Folkore Collections for Children*. Detroit: Neal-Schuman/Gale Research, 1982.

Various authors. *The Oryx Multicultural Folktale Series*. Phoenix: The Oryx Press. Each volume contains around twenty-five variants of the title story, notes about the tale, and classroom activities; see above for examples.

Justifying Storytelling in the Curriculum

Griffin, Barbara Budge. *Students as Storytellers: The Long and the Short of Learning a Story*. Medford, Oregon: Barbara Budge Griffin, 10 S. Kenneway Dr., Medford, OR 97504, 1989. Oregon state student learning objectives are given for each of the eighteen activities in this guide.

Livo, Norma J. and Sandra A. Rietz. "Matrix of Skills and Activities." In *Storytelling Activities*, 125-38. Littleton, Colorado: Libraries Unlimited, 1987. Livo & Rietz list thirty-eight educational skills covered in the story activities in their book. They relate these to Bloom's Taxonomy.

Storytelling for Young Adults

De Vos, Gail. *Storytelling for Young Adults: Technique and Treasury*. Littleton, Colorado: Libraries Unlimited, 1991. Tips for using story with teens, and a selection of suggested stories.

Simmons, Elizabeth Radin. *Student Worlds, Student Words: Teaching Writing through Folklore*. Portsmouth, New Hampshire: Heinemann Educational Books, 1990. Advice on using folklore to start junior high and high school students writing.

Wilson, Evie. "Storytelling Teen Age Folklore." In *Hanging Out at Rocky Creek: Developing Basic Services for Young Adults in Public Libraries*. Metuchen, New Jersey: Scarecrow Press, Inc., 1993. Useful tips on using urban legends with teens.

Collecting Family Folklore

Zeitlin, Steven J., Amy J. Kotkin, and Holly Cutting Baker. *A Celebration of American Family Folklore: Tales and Traditions from the Smithsonian Collection*. New York: Pantheon Books, 1982.

Collecting Oral History

Weitzman, David. *My Backyard History Book.* Boston: Little, Brown, 1975.

Exploring the Folklore of Children

Bronner, Simon J. *American Children's Folklore: A Book of Rhymes, Games, Jokes, Stories, Secret Languages, Beliefs and Camp Legends for Parents, Grandparents, Teachers, Counselors and All Adults Who Were Once Children.* Little Rock: August House Publishers Inc., 1988.

Brunvand, Jan Harold. *The Baby Train and Other Lusty Legends.* New York: W.W. Norton & Co., 1993.

_____. *The Choking Doberman and Other "New" Urban Legends.* New York: W.W. Norton & Co., 1984.

_____. *Curses, Broiled Again! The Hottest Urban Legends Going.* New York: W.W. Norton & Co., 1989.

_____. *The Mexican Pet: More "New" Urban Legends and Some Old Favorites.* New York: W.W. Norton & Co., 1986.

_____. *The Vanishing Hitchhiker: American Urban Legends and Their Meanings.* New York: W.W. Norton & Co., 1981.

Butler, Francelia. *Skipping Around the World: The Ritual Nature of Folk Rhymes.* Hamden, Connecticut: Library Professional Publications, 1988.

MacDonald, Margaret Read. *The Skit Book: 101 Skits from Kids.* Hamden, Connecticut: Linnet Books / The Shoe String Press, 1990.

Paper Folklore (usually for adults)

Dundes, Alan. *Work Hard and You Shall Be Rewarded: Urban Folklore from the Paperwork Empire.* Detroit: Wayne State University Press, 1992 (reprint).

_____. *Never Try to Teach a Pig to Sing: Still More Urban Folklore from the Paperwork Empire.* Detroit: Wayne State University Press, 1991.

Dundes, Alan and Carl R. Pagter. *When You're Up to Your Ass in Alligators: More Urban Folklore from the Paperwork Empire.* Detroit: Wayne State University Press, 1987.

Stories of Ecology

Brody, Ed, Jay Goldspinner, Katie Green, Rona Leventhal and John Porcino, eds. "Living with the Earth." In *Spinning Tales, Weaving Hope: Stories of Peace, Justice and the Environment*, 201-55. Philadelphia: New Society Publishers, 1992.

Caduto, Michael J. and Joseph Bruchac. *Keepers of the Animals: Native*

American Stories and Wildlife Activities for Children. Golden, Colorado: Fulcrum Publishing Inc., 1991.

_____. *Keepers of the Earth: Native American Stories and Environmental Activities for Children*. Golden, Colorado: Fulcrum Publishing Inc., 1988.

Schimmel, Nancy. "Ecology Stories, Songs, and Sources." In *Just Enough to Make a Story*, 50-52. Berkeley, California: Sisters' Choice Press, 1992.

Stories for Peace

Brody, Ed, Jay Goldspinner, Katie Green, Rona Leventhal and John Porcino, eds. "Living with the Earth." In *Spinning Tales, Weaving Hope: Stories of Peace, Justice and the Environment*, 201-55. Philadelphia: New Society Publishers, 1992.

MacDonald, Margaret Read. *Peace Tales: World Folktales to Talk About*. Hamden, Connecticut: Linnet Books / The Shoe String Press, 1992.

Schimmel, Nancy. "Stories in Service to Peace." In *Just Enough to Make a Story*. Berkeley, California: Sisters' Choice Press, 1992.

Stories Featuring Strong Women

Barchers, Suzanne I. *Wise Women: Folk and Fairy Tales from Around the World*. Littleton, Colorado: Libraries Unlimited, 1990.

Carter, Angela. *The Old Wives' Fairy Tale Book*. New York: Pantheon Books, 1990.

McCarty, Toni. *The Skull in the Snow*. New York: Delacorte Press, 1981.

Minard, Rosemary. *Womenfolk and Fairy Tales*. New York: Houghton Mifflin Co., 1975.

Phelps, Ethel Johnston. *The Maid of the North: Feminist Folk Tales from Around the World*. New York: Holt, Rinehart and Winston, 1981.

Schimmel, Nancy. "Active Heroines in Folktales." In *Just Enough to Make a Story*. Berkeley, California: Sisters' Choice Press, 1992.

Zipes, Jack. *Don't Bet on the Prince: Contemporary Feminist Fairy Tales in North America and England*. New York: Methuen, 1986.

Teaching Others to Tell

*A human being who achieves his own truth through the
act and the quality of his doing and his being becomes
the seed of new growth.*

—Laurens van der Post, *A Walk with a White Bushman*

You are but one in a long line of *owners* of this story.
Now that the tale truly *belongs* to you, it is your duty to *pass
it on*. How do you do that? By telling it to others and encouraging them to go tell it. And by *teaching* the tale to others. I
have developed a very simple method for teaching a tale to a
group. It seems to work well with my students. You might try
it with yours.

1. Tell your story. Be sure the audience takes full part in
the story's participatory chants. They are going to have to tell
the entire story soon, so the more they learn on this first
telling, the better. Encourage lots of body language too, if this
is appropriate to the story. The gestures help fix the story in
memory. They can be dropped later if they don't fit the telling
style of this individual.

2. Talk through the entire story again. Point out the tale's
structure as you go. Encourage the class to speak as much of
the story with you as possible. They should already know
chants, repetitive phrases, and dialogues from the first listening.

3. Break your class into small groups. The ideal group
size is three to six students. Assign one person in each group
to begin telling the story. At a given signal from you (hand clap
or bell) each group's beginning teller starts the story: "Once

there was a boy named Jack...."

After a few moments, when you clap your hands again, the beginning teller will stop talking and the person to his or her left will pick up the tale *right where it was left off.* In this way the tale passes around the small group circle. Keep signaling for the next teller to take a turn until the story is done. This gives each person a chance to practice remembering the story in a nonthreatening environment. It also lets them hear others' interpretations of the tale. By the time the students have heard your telling of the story, talked through the story, and retold the story, they essentially *know* the story. Give each student a copy of the tale and encourage them to tell it again as soon as possible and as often as possible.

If your class is focused on performance technique as well as story learning, you can use a similar group telling method to let them retell the story for your class at a later meeting, after they have each developed their own telling of the story. Let five students stand in front of the class. At a signal, the first student begins the tale; at the next signal that student falls silent and another student picks up the story and continues it. In this way several students can perform and receive simple critiquing in a short amount of time, again in a relatively nonthreatening environment.

I use these same techniques when teaching a story to either adults or children. Children, however, are often eager to move the story into dramatic play. After retelling the story in our small groups, we sometimes rework the story once more, this time as story theater. Whether working with children or with adults, it is important to stress that your students should go home and tell the story to someone else.

Now those to whom you *taught* the story are part of the chain of tellers and it is *their* responsibility to *pass it on!*

BIBLIOGRAPHY

Bauer, Caroline Feller. "Teaching Children to Tell Stories." In *Read for the Fun of It: Active Programming with Books for Children*, 126-65. New York: The H.W. Wilson Co., 1992.

Griffin, Barbara Budge. *Student Storyfest: How to Organize a Storytell-*

ing Festival. Medford, Oregon: Barbara Budge Griffin, 10 S. Keeneway Dr., Medford, OR 97504, 1989.

_____. *Students as Storytellers: The Long and the Short of Learning a Story.* Medford, Oregon: Barbara Budge Griffin, 10 S. Keeneway Dr., Medford, OR 97504, 1989. Includes eighteen activities for the classroom designed to teach storytelling skills. Griffin includes a list of learning objectives fulfilled for each activity.

Hamilton, Martha and Mitch Weiss. *Children Tell Stories: A Teaching Guide.* Katonah, New York: Richard C. Owen Publishers Inc., 1990. This excellent advice on learning stories can be used by the beginning teller for *self-instruction* first. Then let this be a starting point for your task of teaching your students to tell.

Herman, Gail N. *Storytelling: A Triad in the Arts.* Mansfield Center, Connecticut: Creative Learning Press, 1986. The aim of this program is to "acquaint interested students with techniques that blend storytelling with other art forms—music, movement, and mime." Interesting advice and useful bibliographies.

Telling it Everywhere

My parents, Charley and Louise Anderson, told stories and historical information to each other all the time, just to remind and refresh themselves.

—Vi Hilbert, Upper Skagit elder in *Haboo: Native American Stories from Puget Sound*

The uses of story are many. Anywhere a group is gathered together with a moment of quietude to listen, or an eagerness to share, story may occur. You really need only two people for story—a teller and a listener. And stories will delight *any* age. Do not limit yourself to one audience; experiment, stretch yourself ... share story *everywhere!*

Who Do You Tell To?

Storytelling to Preschoolers

Storytell to preschoolers? Of course!

They are really never too little to listen. Even babies will often perch transfixed on a parent's lap, their eyes glued to yours as you tell. The preschooler demands more of your attention, of course. Your eyes must be constantly roaming the group, touching *every* face and drawing each listener back into the story over and over again. Nothing is taken for granted with the preschooler.

The group may be enthralled with Jack's encounter with the dog, but before he meets the story's cat a *live* ant may crawl across the floor and take your audience's attention with it. Be flexible. Help the ant out the door and continue the story. Lots of audience involvement helps the preschoolers keep their limited attention fixed on you and the story. Karen really *wants* to hear what happens to Jack next ... but Jenny's hairbow is *so* interesting she has to touch it and Jenny turns around and speaks to her and Karen answers back and ...

To help *both* Jenny and Karen keep their attention on the tale, involve them with verbal responses, movement, or song repeatedly throughout your story. Sometimes my tales *become* audience participation when shared with preschoolers through the sheer desperation of the moment!

Primary School Children

This is the perfect age for story listening. These children are still innocent enough to accept all with wonder yet clever enough to guess at a story's ending and develop a sense of plot. And such creativity! Let them act it, draw it, sing it, dance it! Story follow-ups are a joy with these kids.

Upper Elementary School Children

These listeners are becoming just a *little* worldly, so be sure your stories have enough substance to interest them. Once they get the habit of story listening these students will enjoy almost any well-told tale. They can follow more complicated plots now and appreciate more subtle humour. And their improvisational skills have developed to the point where they can retell or reenact the tales with great effectiveness. Writing skills are developed too by now, so stories can become springboards to help the students' own imaginings spill onto paper.

Junior High and High School Students

Middle-school and high-school audiences can be tough nuts to crack. Of course they love a good tale as much as the rest of us—once they get over their natural instinct that this might be uncool. Look for tales which deal with topics which concern them—love, death, anger, the outsider, youth vs. age. Many fine stories are made to order for this group, but some of the tales which engage teens may be quieter, lengthier, and more difficult to learn than primary school fare.

Several tellers have found urban legends to be a sure-fire entry into storytelling with teens. These simple ghastly tidbits need no special language and work well when retold in your own first-person voice. Read through Jan Harold Brunvand's collections to prime your pump, then start collecting urban legends from your acquaintances. Your most successful tellings will likely come from those about which you can honestly say, "This happened to a *friend of a friend.*" See page 49 for a listing of Brunvand's books, and page 48 for resources on using story with teens.

Another way to ease teens into story listening is to arrange a workshop on storytelling. Drama, child care, or literature classes can easily incorporate a unit on storytelling. Under the guise of learning how to tell, the teens will buy into the most outrageous children's tales with delight. Audience participation tales such as "Jack and the Robbers" and "The Teeny Weeny Bop" turn teen boys into masters of improv. Teenage girls are often too conscious of their image to cut loose at first, but after a few sessions they too begin to give in to story play.

Adults

Well-told personal stories, myths, tales of the fabulous ... many story genres offer keys to our lives. The adult's sense of story is fully developed, the attention span is long, and adults prove eager listeners if you will take the time to seek out and perform the tales we need to hear.

Be mindful that adults need to play, too. The same tale that delights your second-graders may open your adult audience to much-needed play.

Where Shall You Tell?

In the Library

For the first sixty years of this century it was mainly librarians and teachers who kept storytelling in the public eye on this continent. Using story as an enticement to reading, public librarians offered regular story programs. School librarians made storytelling a part of their curriculum. And a few persistent teachers shared story regularly in their classrooms.

In today's stressful workplace storytelling is often abandoned for easier pursuits. Craft programs replace storytelling in the public libraries. Videotapes solve programming needs for the school librarian. Reading aloud seems an adequate effort for the classroom teacher.

But there is still a joy to be found in sharing tales with children in school and public libraries. Story still entices children into books. It still leaves them with positive feelings about the library setting and—not unimportantly—with a generous feeling toward the *librarian!* And of course, exposure to story can't help but improve their own listening and speaking skills. Perhaps equally important is the child's need to hear stories for his or her own emotional and personal development.

So make time for story in your library. Public librarians can include one story in every program. Plan your craft programs to begin with books, poems, and a told story. Tell stories in your preschool storytimes—perhaps not every week, but plug in a good tale now and then. And for special occasions, still offer those lovely "story hour" programs in which children can come to just sit and listen to one fine tale after another.

All this is not as demanding as it sounds. You do not need to learn tons of new stories for each program. Pick a few favorites and keep them in use. Learn one or two new stories every year and add them to your repertoire. An entire "story hour"—more usually around forty-five minutes in length—needs only two or three tales, a song, a couple of poems, and a story stretch. And these can be the same tales that you used in that preschool storytime and told for the craft program last winter. Just recycle and keep telling.

In the Church

Tell stories from the pulpit, in the Sunday school, at family gatherings, with men's and women's groups, with youth groups, at camp. Over the ages, stories have been one of mankind's most effective tools for passing on moral instruction. They still carry this power to impress young minds and stimulate thoughtful consideration.

In the Parks and Recreation Center

Story is a good activity for building group rapport. The shared adventure of a story and the bonding of audience participation help strengthen group identity.

Story can be used to soothe a group, to relax them during their "down time." Or on the other hand, audience partipation story play, like that of the tales in this book, can be used to energize a group, prepare them for action, or simply release energy.

In the Nursing Home or Adult Day-Care Center

Simple, repetitive stories please and energize elderly listeners. Stories which recall their childhood strike a chord in memory. Audience-involving chants and songs can sometimes draw a welcome bit of group play from these audiences.

For nursing homes with a clientele who are infirm but whose memories are intact, your usual repertoire of stories will be well received. Just be sure to speak loudly and slowly enough for all to hear. Hearing loss is a definite factor to be coped with in these settings. A microphone can help when working with groups of twenty or more.

In the Home

Storytelling in the home can be as simple as sharing the events of the day, recounting tales of relative's lives, or sharing a memory from your own childhood. Many parents love to make up fanciful stories at bedtime, letting their own imaginations run wild, often incorporating their own children into the story. The folktale, of course, is still a staple of home storytelling. Begin by telling those you remember hearing as a child and add more tales as you read and discover.

The most important element of home storytelling is that of making time for story. Don't let these special private moments be crowded out of your family's busy life. Look for storytelling opportunities, plan storytelling moments, and *take time to tell.*

BIBLIOGRAPHY

Religious Storytelling

Licht, Jacob. *Storytelling in the Bible.* Jerusalem: The Magnes Press, The Hebrew University, 1978. For the serious bibical scholar. An analysis of the storytelling techniques of the Bible's authors.

White, William R. *Stories for Telling: A Treasury for Christian Story-tellers.* Minneapolis: Augsburg Fortress Publishers, 1986. Useful selection of tales and a chapter on "Storytelling in the Ministry."

Williams, Michael E. *The Storyteller's Companion to the Bible. Volume One. Genesis.* Nashville: Abingdon Press, 1991.

_____. *The Storytellers' Companion to the Bible. Volume Two. Exodus-Joshua.* Nashville: Abingdon Press, 1992. This and the entry above include story selections from *The Revised English Bible,* comments on each story, a sample elaborated retelling, and a few related Midrashim for each.

Story Programs for the Public Library

Baker, Augusta and Ellin Greene. *Storytelling: Art and Technique.* New York: R.R. Bowker, 1977.

Bauer, Caroline Feller. *Celebrations.* New York: The H.W. Wilson Co., 1985.

_____. *Handbook for Storytellers.* Chicago: American Library Association, 1977.

_____. *This Way to Books.* New York: The H.W. Wilson Co., 1983.

De Wit, Dorothy. *Children's Faces Looking Up: Program Building for the Storyteller.* Chicago: American Library Association, 1979. Suggested story groupings on many themes and a chapter on "The Elements of Programming."

Iarusso, Marilyn. *Stories: A List of Stories to Tell and Read Aloud.* New York: New York Public Library, 1990.

Shaw, Spencer G. "First Steps: Storytime With Young Listeners." In *Start Early for an Early Start: You and the Young Child*, edited by Ferne Johnson, 41-64. Chicago: American Library Association, 1976.

Telling Stories to Adults

Chinen, Allan B. *In the Ever After: Fairy Tales and the Second Half of Life.* Wilmette, Illinois: Chiron Publications, 1989. Fifteen traditional tales featuring elders. Each accompanied by Jungian analysis. An interesting book with good tale selection.

_____. *Once Upon a Midlife: Classic Stories and Mythic*

Tales to Illuminate the Middle Years. Los Angeles: Jeremy P. Tarcher Inc., 1992.

Schimmel, Nancy. "Sources for Stories to Tell Adults." In *Just Enough to Make a Story*, 36-38. Berkeley, California: Sisters' Choice Press, 1992. Bibliography and comments.

Using Traditional Storytelling in the Home

Allison, Christine. *I'll Tell You a Story, I'll Sing You A Song: A Parent's Guide to the Fairy Tales, Fables, Songs, and Rhymes of Childhood.* New York: Delacorte Press, 1987. Good advice for the beginning teller in boxed columns sprinkled throughout the book. However, you will find more tellable versions of most of these tales elsewhere.

MacDonald, Margaret Read. *A Parent's Guide to Storytelling.* New York: HarperCollins Publishers, 1994. Useful advice for the parent teller plus easy-to-tell stories.

Pellowski, Anne. *The Family Storytelling Handbook: How to Use Stories, Anecdotes, Rhymes, Handkerchiefs, Paper, and Other Objects to Enrich Your Family Traditions.* New York: MacMillan Inc., 1987.

_____. *Hidden Stories in Plants: Unusual and Easy-to-Tell Stories from Around the World Together with Creative Things to Do While Telling Them.* New York: MacMillan Inc., 1990. Simple plant crafts and accompanying stories.

Stories the Parent Creates for the Child

Brett, Doris. *Annie Stories: A Special Kind of Storytelling.* New York: Workman Publishing Co., 1986. The jacket copy says these created stories "allow children under ten to explore situations in an engaging, non-threatening way through the experiences of an imaginary boy or girl much like themselves." Written by a clinical psychologist.

Collins, Chase. *Tell Me a Story: Creating Bedtime Tales Your Children Will Dream On.* Boston: Houghton Mifflin Co., 1992. Stimulating the imagination to create your own bedtime stories.

Moore, Robin. *Awakening the Hidden Storyteller: How to Build a Storytelling Tradition in Your Family.* Boston: Shambhala Publications Inc., 1991. Creative visualization and inner journeys in search of one's guardian animal and the hidden teller within. The exercises are to be shared by the entire family.

Exploring Family Folklore

Zeitlin, Steven J., Amy J. Kotkin, and Holly Cutting Baker. *A Celebration of American Family Folklore: Tales and Traditions from the Smithsonian Collection.* New York: Pantheon Books, 1982.

Finding the Story

The tales are like rays of light, taking their colors from the medium through which they pass.

—W.A. Bone, *Children's Stories and How to Tell Them*

You are eager to focus on a story for your listeners. To begin you must find a story you *want* to tell. Where do you go to find a story? To a *storyteller*. Whether that teller is standing before you or is recorded in print, remember that this tale passed to you through another's telling.

1. Find a storyteller in the written word.

Storytelling is an *oral* tradition. Print, Midas-like, declares a tale golden but freezes it into lifeless eternity. After generations of flowing, malleable, from tongue to tongue, the tale finds itself entrapped in *one* form. It is up to you to release the tale and set it free to flow again.

Somewhere behind that printed text stands a teller. To effectively *re*tell you must reach back and touch that teller. This is not always easy. Many of our printed texts have been rewritten by authors with no ear for the spoken word. Early ethnologists often took down barebones story plots from their informants. Contemporary authors have used these plots as the bases for story collections. Rewritten with an eye to literary rather than oral considerations—and sometimes altered through vocabulary control or purification for a child audience—these tales move farther and farther from the teller's voice. You may recognize the seed of a good story in such collections, but trying to put that tale back into the spoken word is difficult.

Collections by Storyteller/Authors

For easiest tale selection, try those stories which have been chosen by authors who are themselves storytellers. These tales, which come from the working repertoires of tellers, have already been refined for oral telling. These tellers have selected from their own repertoire tales which tell well. Here the author has already done the work of returning the story from frozen print to oral telling. Some of these collections even include notes with suggestions for telling the tales effectively. See the bibliography for collections by Anne Pellowski, Ruth Sawyer, and other author/tellers.

Storyteller/Author/Collector

Especially useful are those collections prepared by author/tellers who have collected tales directly from traditional tellers. I use the term "traditional teller" to refer to those folks who have learned their stories orally through elders in their own culture. Each of us may be a bearer of some tales from our own tradition, but most of us are basically "revivalist" tellers. We discover the tales in print and "revive" them.

Diane Wolkstein and Richard Chase are two tellers who collected from living informants. They then honed these tales for their own audiences through repeated tellings before selecting those which might best serve us. Note that they do not reproduce the *exact* words of the traditional teller throughout the tale. Though they stay very close to their sources, they have reshaped the tales slightly to work with our audiences.

Collectors Working Within Their Own Cultures

We are fortunate to have a few collections prepared by tellers working within their *own* cultures. Ethnomusicologists Moses Serawadda of Uganda and Adjai Robinson of Sierra Leone, and the Burmese folklorist Maung Htin Aung, for example, have produced delightful collections that share their cultures with our children.

However, being a member of a culture does not necessarily mean that an author has an ear for the oral tale. Evaluate each collection you discover carefully.

Folklorists' Field Collections

Today's folklorists are interested not only in the tale but also in the *teller*. Recent field collections give us verbatim transcriptions of the teller's words. These collectors also tell us about the tale-telling *event*. They discuss the teller's performance style, the audience response, and the function of the tale for audience and teller. Through such collections we can come closer to those tellers who bestow their tales on us. The works of Dennis Tedlock, Peter Seitel, and others offer a glance into the world of the folk teller. Not all of these tales will work for your audience, but these books will put you in touch with the living tradition of tale telling which you now join.

Finding the Teller through Media

Many professional tellers are available to you on audiotape or videotape. It is hard to bring life to words on a printed page, but once you *hear* another teller speak them, the tale may suddenly live for you. Professional tellers who write their own material—instead of using folk literature—often do not want their material retold. But the *folktale* belongs to no one teller. Feel free to take inspiration from another teller's taped rendition in creating your own version. (For discussions of such issues of storytelling rights, permissions, and copyrights, see items in the bibliography on page 72.) For one list of tapes and video material write for the catalog of the National Association for the Preservation and Perpetuation of Storytelling (NAPPS, P.O. Box 309, Jonesborough, TN 37659).

Finding a Live Teller

It is likely that storytellers live in your community. A little sleuthing may be necessary to find them. Watch the local papers for announcements of storytelling events, ask your local children's librarian for leads, and perk up your ears for news of traditional tellers. You may well have some living treasures right next door.

Many areas have storytelling organizations that meet regularly to exchange stories or present programs. See pages 97-

99 for information on the national networks that can help you locate such groups in your area.

2. Find a storyteller whose style matches yours.

Each teller will speak with a unique voice. By listening to many tellers you will happen onto a few whose style suits you especially well. Let those tellers be your mentors. Examine the sources from which they select tales. Listen to their tapes over and over to understand their techniques. Do not *imitate* but do draw inspiration from those whose telling pleases you.

3. Investigate those cultures whose tales excite you.

You may find that certain cultures produce tales that give you special pleasure. Syd Lieberman's Jewish tales may delight you; or the spunky, slightly ribald Haitian characters of Diane Wolkstein's *Magic Orange Tree* may insist that you tell about them. Perhaps the complex imagery of Padraic Colum's *Legends of Hawaii* will startle your imagination.

Wherever you find a spark, take a clue. Here may lie buried treasure. After reading *The Magic Orange Tree* I went straight to the library and ordered every collection of Haitian folktales available. If the Haitians were telling such wonderful tales, I wanted to see more.

Know that your local library can order through interlibrary loan (ILL) almost any book for which you can provide author and title. If it isn't in the catalog, just ask your librarian if they can get it through ILL. Most libraries can.

4. Start a story bank.

As you read and listen, start a list of stories you might want to tell some day. In addition to the story title, book title, and author, it is useful to jot down the catalog number of the book and note the library where you found it. To make certain I have the tale at hand when I want it, I photocopy those tales that appeal to me and keep a file of "Tales to Learn Someday."

Since searching for the "perfect" tale is by far the most time-consuming part of tale preparation, a handy file of pre-selected tales will serve you well in the future. Often a potentially good tale will not quite suit your need or mood of the moment. Just pop it into your folder for another day.

BIBLIOGRAPHY

Collections with Texts Close to Their Oral Traditions

These will be easier to retell since they were written down in the way the traditional teller spoke them.

Chase, Richard. *Grandfather Tales.* Boston: Houghton Mifflin Co., 1948.

_____. *The Jack Tales.* Boston: Houghton Mifflin Co., 1943. Collected by Chase from friends in the Appalachian Mountains. Retold by Chase, who used these stories in his own repertoire.

Jacobs, Joseph. *English Folk and Fairy Tales.* New York: The G.P. Putnam's Sons, c. 1898.

_____. *More English Folk and Fairy Tales.* New York: The Putnam Berkley Group Inc., c. 1898. These tales, collected by nineteenth-century folklorists, have changed little from their original tellings.

Robinson, Adjai. *Singing Tales of Africa.* New York: Charles Scribner's Sons, 1974. Tales from Sierra Leone, Nigeria, and Ghana retold by a Sierra Leone author who is a storyteller. His book includes music for all songs.

Serwadda, W. Moses. *Songs and Stories from Uganda.* New York: Thomas Y. Crowell, 1974. Serwadda is a Mukunja musician and storyteller. After receiving his master's degree in African dance from the University of Ghana, he began teaching with the Department of Music and Dance at Makerere University in Kampala. His book includes music for all songs along with the words in both English and Luganda.

Tracy, Hugh. *The Lion on the Path and Other African Stories.* New York: Praeger Publishers, 1967. Tracy is a British ethnomusicologist who has spent much of his career in Zimbabwe. He includes musical notation for the songs. Two of these story-songs are performed by Tracy's son, ethnomusicologist Andrew Tracy, in *Mapandangare: The Great Baboon* (Studio City, California: Filmfair, 1978) and *The Dancing Lion* (Studio City, California: Filmfair, 1978). These are available in both 16 mm and videotape.

Collections by Storyteller / Authors

These tales are chosen from the repertoires of school, library, and professional storytellers. The tellings worked well with their audiences. You may enjoy them too.

Bryan, Ashley. *Beat the Story-Drum, Pum, Pum.* New York: Atheneum

Publishers, 1980. Though Bryan is primarily an artist, his extensive experience as a performer of his own work informs his storyteller's ear.

Chapman, Jean. *Tell Me Another Tale: Stories, Verses, Songs and Things to Do.* Sydney: Hodder and Stoughton, 1976.

Fitzgerald, Burdette S. *World Tales for Creative Dramatics and Storytelling.* Englewood Cliffs, New Jersey: Prentice-Hall Press, 1962. More than one hundred multicultural tales. Most are very good for storytelling.

Hayes, Joe. *A Heart Full of Turquoise: Pueblo Indian Tales.* Santa Fe, New Mexico: Mariposa Publishing Co., 1988. Pueblo tales retold from anthropological sources by a non-Indian teller with a good ear for story.

MacDonald, Margaret Read. *Look Back and See: Twenty Lively Tales for Gentle Tellers.* New York: The H.W. Wilson Co., 1991. Audience participation folktales with a gentle slant. This multi-ethnic collection features tales from twenty cultures.

_____. *Peace Tales: World Folktales to Tall About.* Hamden, Connecticut: Linnet Books / The Shoe String Press, 1992. Some to tell, some to talk about. By this author and other tellers.

_____. *Twenty Tellable Tales: Audience Participation Folktales for the Beginning Storyteller.* New York: The H.W. Wilson Co., 1986. Easy-to-learn folktales. Includes several longtime favorites of school and library storytellers.

_____. *When the Lights Go Out: Twenty Scary Tales to Tell.* New York: The H.W. Wilson Co., 1988. A bit of spooky fare for every audience from not-so-scary preschool fare to the truly creepy.

Miller, Teresa. *Joining In: an Anthology of Audience Participation Stories and How to Tell Them,* edited by Norma Livo. Compiled by Teresa Miller with assistance from Anne Pellowski. Cambridge, Massachusetts: Yellow Moon Press, 1988. Audience participation stories from eighteen professional storytellers. Margin notes tell how the teller worked with the audience to carry forward the tale. Beginning tellers can learn much from reading these marginal notes and noticing techniques used by these tellers.

Pellowski, Anne. *The Family Storytelling Handbook: How to Use Stories, Anecdotes, Rhymes, Handkerchiefs, Paper, and Other Objects to Enrich Your Family Traditions.* New York: MacMillan, Inc. 1987.

_____. *The Story Vine: A Source Book of Unusual and Easy-to-Tell Stories from Around the World.* New York: MacMillan, 1984. Pellowski, former librarian with the United States Committee for UNICEF has collected from around the world string stories, drawing stories, object stories, finger-play stories—a useful assortment of entertaining and easy-to-execute story material. Good repertoire stretchers for the beginning teller. Easy to learn and sure to please.

Sierra, Judy and Robert Kaminski. *Multicultural Folktales: Stories to Tell Young Children.* Phoenix: The Oryx Press, 1991. Includes stories for the very young, three to five years old.

Tashjian, Virginia. *Juba This and Juba That: Story Hour Stretches for Large and Small Groups.* Boston: Little, Brown & Co., 1969.

_____. *With a Deep Sea Smile: Story Hour Stretches for Large and Small Groups.* Boston: Little, Brown & Co., 1974.

Over the years, several library storytellers have published collections of their favorite stories for telling. Look in your library for collections by Augusta Baker, Pura Belpre, Eileen Colwell, Mary Gould Davis, Mae Durham, Ellin Greene, Jeanne Hardendorff, Virginia Haviland, Eulalie Steinmetz Ross, and Ruth Sawyer.

Good Sources for the Traditional British Nursery Tale

You probably already know these stories—The Little Red Hen, The Gingerbread Boy, The Three Bears ... Refresh your memory and add these to your repertoire. Young children still love them.

Hutchinson, Veronica S. *Chimney Corner Stories: Tales for Little Children.* Hamden, Connecticut: Linnet Books, 1992 (reprint).

_____. *Fireside Stories.* New York: Minton & Balch, 1927.

Richardson, Frederick. *Great Children's Stories.* Chicago: Rand McNally & Co., 1923. Reprint 1972.

To Search for Tales from a Specific Culture

If you decide you would like to read more collections from a certain culture area, begin by checking the subject catalog in your local library. Try the subject heading "Folklore—China," for example. To compile a more lengthy bibliography of materials from that culture, check the subject index to Books in Print. *For a listing of collections from various areas see the "Ethnic and Geographical Index" in* The Storyteller's Sourcebook *by Margaret Read MacDonald (Detroit: Neal-Schuman / Gale Research, 1982).*

Two useful book series may have included collections from the culture area in which you are interested.

• The **Folktales of the World** series, edited by Richard M. Dorson, offers a selection of folktales from each country. Motif and type numbers are provided along with scholarly comparative notes for each tale. An essay discussing the history of folktale research in that country introduces each volume. Each is prepared by a noted folktale scholar from that country.

Briggs, Katharine M. and Ruth L. Tongue, editors. *Folktales of England.* Chicago: University of Chicago Press, 1965.

Christiansen, Reidar Th., ed. *Folktales of Norway.* Chicago: University of Chicago Press, 1964.

Degh, Linda, ed. *Folktales of Hungary.* Chicago: University of Chicago Press, 1965.

Eberhard, Wolfram, ed. *Folktales of China.* Chicago: University of Chicago Press, 1965.

El-Shamy, Hasan M., ed. *Folktales of Egypt.* Chicago: University of Chicago Press, 1979.

Massignon, Genevieve, ed. *Folktales of France.* Chicago: University of Chicago Press, 1968.

Megas, Georgios A., ed. *Folktales of Greece.* Chicago: University of Chicago Press, 1970.

Noy, Dov, ed. *Folktales of Israel.* Chicago: University of Chicago Press, 1963.

O'Sullivan, Sean, ed. *Folktales of Ireland.* Chicago: University of Chicago Press, 1966.

Paredes, Americo, ed. *Folktales of Mexico.* Chicago: University of Chicago Press, 1970.

Pino-Saavedra, Yolanda, ed. *Folktales of Chile.* Chicago: University of Chicago Press, 1968.

Ranke, Kurt, ed. *Folktales of Germany.* Chicago: University of Chicago Press, 1968.

Seki, Keigo, ed. *Folktales of Japan.* Chicago: University of Chicago Press, 1963.

• **The Pantheon Fairy Tale and Folklore Library** series includes several useful collections from world folk literature. Volumes are hefty, including up to two hundred tales. Some include brief tale notes. Here are a few titles from this series:

Abrahams, Roger D. *Afro-American Folktales.* New York: Pantheon Books, 1985.

Bushnaq, Inea. *Arab Folktales.* New York: Pantheon Books, 1986.

Calvino, Italo. *Italian Folktales.* New York: Pantheon Books, 1981.

Erdoes, Richard and Alfonso Ortiz. *American Indian Myths and Legends.* New York: Pantheon Books, 1984.

Weinreich, Beatrice Silverman and Leonard Wolf. *Yiddish Folktales.* New York: Pantheon Books, 1988.

Learning from Picture Books

The beginning teller may find a shortcut to tale learning by selecting a well-written folktale in picture book format. The illustrations in the picture book will help fix the story in your imagination. Share this first by reading it aloud to several different groups of children. Then, once the tale has begun to fit you, put the book away and tell it. This technique works well for school librarians who see many classes each week.

Here are a few recent picture books that lend themselves to telling. For a lengthier list see "The Picture Book as Story Source" on pp. 204-08 of Margaret Read MacDonald's Twenty Tellable Tales *(New York: H.W. Wilson Co., 1986).*

Aardema, Verna. *Traveling to Tondo: A Tale of the Nkundo of Zaire.* Illus. by Will Hillenbrand. New York: Alfred A. Knopf, 1991.

Ata, Te. *Baby Rattlesnake.* Adapted by Lynn Moroney. Illus. by Veg Reisburg. San Francisco: Children's Book Press, 1989.

DeFelice, Cynthia C. *The Dancing Skeleton.* Illus. by Robert Andrew Parker. New York: MacMillan, 1989.

DePaola, Tomie, *Fin M'Coul: The Giant of Knockmany Hill.* New York: Holiday House, 1981.

Kimmel, Eric A. *Anansi and the Moss Covered Rock.* Illus. by Janet Stevens. New York: Holiday House, 1988.

Stamm, Claus. *Three Strong Women: A Tale from Japan.* Illus. by Jean and Mou-Sien Tseng. New York: Viking Press, 1990.

Xiong, Blia. *Nine-in-One Grr! Grr!* Adapted by Cathy Spagnoli. Illus. by Nancy Hom. San Francisco: Children's Book Press, 1989.

Lists of Tales for Telling

Books about storytelling often include lists of suggested stories for telling. Two recently updated lists which you may find useful are:

Iarusso, Marilyn. *Stories: A List of Stories to Tell and Read Aloud.* New York: New York Public Library, 1990.

Schimmel, Nancy. "Sisters' Choice." In *Just Enough to Make a Story.* Berkeley, California: Sisters' Choice Press, 1992.

Learn by Listening

Many audio- and videotapes featuring storytellers are available. Listen to these for devices which may work in your own telling. Do not imitate such tapes, but draw inspiration from them as you develop a style that fits your own persona. Beginning tellers often find it easy to add to their repertoire by learning stories other tellers have perfected through repeated listenings to story tapes. This is a useful start-up activity for most beginning tellers, but keep in mind that those pieces are sometimes thought of as personal property by the tellers who made the tapes. You would need to receive permission from that teller if you begin to tell for profit later in your career.

Here is a brief selection of tapes and videos I find useful for beginners. Your public library will have these and many more.

AUDIOTAPES

Greene, Ellin. *Elis Piddock Skips in Her Sleep*. Albany, New York: A Gentle Wind, 1984. A fine public library storyteller shares a classic Eleanor Farjeon story.

Hayes, Joe. *A Heart Full of Turquoise: Pueblo Indian Tales*. Santa Fe, New Mexico: Trails West Publishing, n.d. Simple, effective tellings.

Lieberman, Syd. *Joseph the Tailor and Other Jewish Tales*. Evanston, Illinois: Syd Lieberman, 1988. Told before a live audience.

Lipman, Doug. *Tell It With Me*. Albany, New York: A Gentle Wind, n.d. Tales for younger children, told to a squiggly class.

VIDEOTAPES

Davis, Donald. *The Crack of Dawn*. The H.W. Wilson Co. American Storytelling Series, 1986. Creating story from pieces of memory.

Freeman, Barbara and Connie Regan-Blake. *No News*. New York: The H.W. Wilson Co. American Storytelling Series, 1986. Dynamic examples of tandem telling.

Rubright, Lynn. *Baked Potatoes*. New York: The H.W. Wilson Co. American Storytelling Series, 1986. How to turn a simple incident into an engaging narrative.

Seago, Billy. *Stories from the Attic: The Greedy Cat*. Seattle: Sign-a-Vision, 1987.

_____. *Stories from the Attic: The House that Jack Built*. Seattle: Sign-a-Vision, 1987.

_____. *Stories from the Attic: The Magic Pot*. Seattle: Sign-a-Vision, 1987.
    Stories in sign language—available in ASL or Signed English—with voice-over. Billy comments on the use of body language and facial expression to convey meaning in storytelling.

Rights, Permissions, and Copyrights

You infringe on someone else's copyright when you use their material to put money in your pocket. If you are telling your own version of a folktale, or if you are telling a literary work in an educational setting for no fee, you are not violating copyright. However, tellers who have worked hard to perfect a tale may not be happy to hear their hard work mimicked by others, so personal consideration should be exercised. Once you begin telling for a fee, or producing tapes or books for sale, permission to use literary material is absolutely required.

Skinrud, Michael E. "Copyright and Storytelling." In *The National Storytelling Journal*, Winter 1984, 14-19. (Available in reprint for $6.00 from NAPPS, P.O. Box 309, Jonesborough, TN 37659.)

Looking at Stories Critically

A gift for selection ... comes partly out of experience,
the innumerable times of trying out a story and
summing up the consequences. But the secret of the gift
lies in the sixth sense of the true storyteller. Here is an
indefinable something that acts as does the nose for the
winetaster, the fingertips for the textile expert, an
absolute pitch for the musician. I think one may be
born with this; But it is far more likely to become
ingrained after years of experience.

—Ruth Sawyer, *The Way of the Storyteller*

To develop an eye and an ear for story you will want to read widely. I suggest that you bring home a pile of fine literary story collections and dabble in them until you are steeped in their language. These stories are too difficult for the beginner to tackle, since they must be learned word for word if they are to be retold properly. But wrapping yourself in their lovely rhythm and wording will help you develop a sense for the well-crafted phrase.

Read Sandburg, Farjeon, Kipling, Andersen, Colum. Read them aloud and listen.

Next read among collections prepared by contemporary folklorists that present the tales of living traditional tellers in ethnopoetic form. The collector has tried to set the words on the page in English translation in a way that portrays the actual performance of that teller. This is the sound of the oral teller in performance. Examine these collections carefully.

Again, read them aloud and listen.

Try the work of contemporary folklorists such as Dennis Tedlock *(Finding the Center)*, Peter Seitel (*See So That We May See)*, or Joan M. Tenenbaum (*Dena-ina Sukdu-a: Traditional Stories of the Tanaina)*. Or read Joseph Jacob's *English Folk and Fairy Tales*, Diane Wolkstein's *The Magic Orange Tree and Other Haitian Folktales*, or Richard Chase's *Grandfather Tales*.

An innate sense for the rhythm and flow of a tale can be gained only through listening again and again. As a beginning teller you will select tales which are already well-written for telling, but later you may want to retell stories from less skillfully written sources. It is then that this grounding in fine story collections will be essential.

Avoiding the Simplified Story

Our children's folktale collections are often rewritings drawing on tale plots found in anthropological collections. They vary with the skill of the author. Beware of oversimplified stories. One of the most common horrors of folktale rewriting is that of the author who writes all of the loveliness out of the tale with the false assumption that this makes it more accessible to young children. Preschool children need to hear fine language just as much as the rest of us. The fact that they haven't heard it before just makes it that much *more* important that they hear it now.

Here are two segments from "The Gingerbread Boy"— one from an author with a proven ear for language, the other from an educator with an eye for simplification. Never deprive your children of a tale's potential by giving them such "simplified" versions.

Paul Galdone's *The Gingerbread Boy* reads:

> She ran to the oven and opened the door.
> Up jumped the Gingerbread Boy.
> He hopped down onto the floor,
> ran across the kitchen,
> out of the door,

across the garden,
through the gate,
and down the road as fast as
his gingerbread legs could carry him.

The little old woman and the little old man
    ran after him,
shouting: "Stop! Stop, little Gingerbread
    Boy!"

The Gingerbread Boy looked back and
    laughed and called out:
"Run! Run! Run!
Catch me if you can!
You can't catch me!
I'm the Gingerbread Boy,
I am! I am!"
And they couldn't catch him.[1]

A simplified version by Jean Warren in her *Totline* January-February 1989 issue reads:

Suddenly it stood up, hopped out of
the pan, then jumped to the floor and ran
out the door.
    As it ran past the wife, she heard it cry,
"Run, run, fast as you can, you can't catch
me, I'm the Pancake Man."
    The wife tried to catch him but she
couldn't.[2]

This simplified version for small children then deletes the pancake man's chanting retorts for the rest of the tale, continuing simply. "He ran past the daughter but the daughter couldn't catch him. He ran past the farmer but the farmer couldn't catch him." The reteller adds a dog and a cat and eliminates the horse, threshers and mowers. The fox is also eliminated and the Pancake Man is left running at the end. "He ran and ran and ran. Has anybody seen that Pancake Man?"
    My quarrel is not with the altered ending, but with the

elimination of the rhythmic joy found in the bouncy tellings of almost all folk versions of this tale. Galdone understands this rhythm well and capitalizes on it. Warren ignores it.

Avoiding the Overwritten Story

Many of the folktale collections you will find on your library shelves have been retold by authors with an eye to literary form rather than an ear for the oral tale. These authors will have added lengthy descriptive passages, padding the simple oral tale with verbiage to meet literary criteria. This may make for a fine tale to read aloud, but it does not move easily back into the storytelling format.

Look, for example, at the opening for two versions of "The Tongue Cut Sparrow." The first was prepared by a children's author:

> It was autumn, and the dawn was breaking. The forest was afire with the red of maple trees; the cranes glided down to the watery rice-fields to dab for their morning meal; the croaks of the bull-frogs rumbled from the river banks; and Mount Fuji, wreathed in clouds, breathed idly and contentedly on the distant skyline. It was a season and a morning dear to the old woodcutter's heart, and neither his poverty nor the sharp tongue of his irascible wife disturbed his tranquillity and happiness as slowly, with bent back and grasping a stout staff in his hand, he tramped through the forest to cut the day's fuel.[3]

The second passage gives us the words of a folk teller, translated by Japanese scholar Keigo Seki:

> Well, this was long ago. There was an old man and his wife. One day the old man went to the mountains to cut firewood.[4]

Rather than work at cutting tales back to a tellable form, look for tales such as Seki's which have not been so far removed from the storyteller's tongue. Bibliographies for this chapter and for "Finding the Story" (page 67) suggest several such collections.

Finding Other Variants of Your Story

Sometimes you will discover a story that excites you, but the language or the story development seems not quite as you would like it. If you are working with a folktale, you may be able to locate other tellings of the same tale. No two tellers give the story in exactly the same way. Another teller's version may suit your needs better than the one you have in hand. Indexes are available to help you search for these tale variants. Here are two indexes which you will find in most public libraries:

- *The Storyteller's Sourcebook: A Subject, Title, and Motif-Index to Folklore Collections for Children* by Margaret Read MacDonald (Detroit: Neal-Schuman / Gale Research, 1982).

    The Storyteller's Sourcebook allows you to search by story title or through an extensive story subject index. This book is arranged according to the classification system of the Stith Thompson *Motif-Index of Folk-Literature* (Bloomington: Indiana University Press, 1966). This means that similar tales appear side by side in the motif-index. So once you find your tale, you can also scan information about *similar* tales from other cultures. Each tale is described and variants from around the world are cited. For tellers who become seriously hooked on folktale searches, there are many scholarly type and motif indexes arranged like *The Storyteller's Sourcebook*. Some of these are listed in *Twenty Tellable Tales* by the same author (New York: The H.W. Wilson Co., 1986).

    You will want to get your hands on *The Storyteller's Sourcebook* and browse through it for a while to become familiar with its arrangement. Tellers enjoy reading through the pages of tale descriptions and wondering about the many variants of their favorite tales. For example, thirty-six variants of the Cinderella story are described.

• *Index to Fairy Tales: Including Folklore, Legends, and Myths in Collections* by Norma Olin Ireland and Joseph W. Sprug (Metuchen, New Jersey: Scarecrow Press, various).

This series originated as *Index to Fairy Tales, Myths, and Legends* by Mary Huse Eastman (Westwood, Massachusetts: Faxon, various). These indexes were begun in 1926 by Eastman and have been updated periodically by Ireland. The early volumes have tale title entries only, but since the 1949-1972 edition, a subject index has been included. These indexes include neither a motif approach nor tale descriptions, but they do include some titles which are not included in *The Storyteller's Sourcebook*.

Retelling Your Own Story

When, after reading, listening, and telling for a while, you need to begin rewriting stories for your own telling use, you may want to check with the advice of other tellers on this difficult task. See the bibliography at the end of this chapter for sources which may help you.

Exploring Other Genres

This book starts you on the road to storytelling with a few simple folktales. These are tales that my listeners have loved, but they may or may not match your personal needs. Examine the many materials listed in the bibliographies here and listen to tapes of other tellers.

Personal stories

Certainly you will want to add some personal stories to your repertoire. If you work with children there is much you can share with them informally from your own past that will have meaning and interest for them. Whether you polish this material into "stories" or simply share them as informal memories, make a point of searching your past for material which should be passed on.

One way to shape such material into a "story" is to share

it with several different friends informally in conversation. As the story begins to take shape and become more "tellable," set aside time to work with the story. Ask yourself what *you* want the story to carry to the listener. Try various ways to achieve your ends and select those which seem to be most effective. Tape your own oral telling of the story, transcribe it, and edit the tale in transcript form. Different aspects of the tale will emerge as you transfer it from oral form to written and back to oral again.

Literary stories

You will definitely want to add a few literary pieces to your repertoire. These will require memorization and hard work, but they are worth it. Some tellers will find these pieces more fulfilling than the telling of folktales and will build an entire repertoire of literary material. Others will prefer the more open-ended story-play allowed by the folktale. Whichever genre you prefer, know that your selection is good: if you *enjoy* it, it is right for *your* telling.

The telling of myths

The world's mythology is a fascinating source of story-lore. Unfortunately for beginners, most of these tales are available only in literary retellings. Adapting them for an oral telling requires a skilled ear and a clear eye. Read widely in collections of myth and listen to other tellers to observe the choices they have made in adapting this material for telling. Then be prepared to devote serious critical effort to your tale preparation as you begin to tell in this genre.

Historical stories

This story genre also requires considerable preparation. The stories do not come to you "ready-to-tell." Often, however, it is possible to find pieces of the story you wish to tell already framed charmingly by local elders. Published oral histories are rich in such material, as are some local histories. Letters may also bear material which moves easily to the tongue. By carefully selecting and combining such material, several storytellers have produced intriguing and moving historical storytellings.

In defense of the folktale

My colleagues sometimes suggest that those elaborate, soul-searched, personal stories and the hard-honed literary pieces which they construct and perform for adults are a higher art form, somehow on a different plane from the work of simply "telling stories to children." Nonsense. Art is not judged by "difficulty in preparation" or "length of presentation." Art is judged by the ear and the heart. A simply told parable may stand above all of these elaborately developed twenty-minute recitations. And the simple "children's" folktale which you carry may well be the artistic gem of another culture's *adult* community.

Discover the form of storying that pleases *you*. Then cherish it and carry it into the world with *pride*.

NOTES

[1] Paul Galdone, *The Gingerbread Boy* (New York: Clarion Books, 1975), 11-13.

[2] "The Pancake Man," adapted by Jean Warren, in *Totline* January-February 1989, 10.

[3] Helen and William McAlpine, *Japanese Tales and Legends* (New York: Henry A. Walek, 1950), 188.

[4] Keigo Seki, *Folktales of Japan* (Chicago: University of Chicago Press, 1963), 115.

BIBLIOGRAPHY

Reading to Develop an Ear for Fine Language

Andersen, Hans Christian. *Andersen's Fairy Tales.* Trans. by Mrs. E.V. Lucas and Mrs. H.B. Paull. New York: Grosset & Dunlap Publishers, 1945.

Colum, Padraic. *Legends of Hawaii.* New Haven: Yale University Press, 1937.

Farjeon, Eleanor. *Martin Pippin in the Daisy Field.* Philadelphia: J.B. Lippincott Co., 1937.

Kennedy, Richard. *Richard Kennedy: Collected Stories.* New York: Harper & Row, 1987.

Kipling, Rudyard. *Just So Stories.* Garden City, New York: Doubleday, 1912.

Pyle, Howard. *Pepper and Salt: Seasoning for Young Folk.* New York: Harper & Row, 1913.

Sandburg, Carl. *Rootabaga Stories.* New York: Harcourt, Brace & World, 1950.

Reading to Develop an Ear for the Oral Telling

Read all collections mentioned under "Collections with Texts Close to Their Oral Traditions" (p. 67). Read also these collections by contemporary folklorists. They present the tales in ethnopoetic form, allowing the reader to sense where the teller breathed, added emphasis, or dropped voice.

Seitel, Peter. *See So That We May See: Performance and Interpretations of Traditional Tales from Tanzania.* Bloomington: Indiana University Press, 1980.

Tedlock, Dennis. *Finding the Center: Narrative Poetry of the Zuni Indians.* Lincoln: University of Nebraska Press, 1972.

Tenenbaum, Joan M. and Mary J. McGary. *Dena'ina Sukdu'a: Traditional Stories of the Tanaina Athabaskans.* Fairbanks: Alaska Native Language Center, University of Alaska Press, 1984.

And Read in These Excellent Children's Collections Too

Fillmore, Parker. *The Shepherd's Nosegay: Stories from Finland and Czechoslovakia.* New York: Harcourt, Brace & Company, 1919. Reprint c. 1958.

Hamilton, Virginia. *The People Could Fly: American Black Folktales.* New York: Alfred A. Knopf Inc., 1985.

Walker, Barbara K. *A Treasury of Turkish Tales for Children.* Hamden, Connecticut: Linnet Books, 1988.

Advice on Finding Your Story

Smith, Jimmy Neil. "Discovering Your Story." In *Homespun: Tales from America's Favorite Storytellers*, 305-18. New York: Crown Publishing Group, 1988.

Researching Tale Variants

Ashliman, D.L. *A Guide to Folktales in the English Language: Based on the Aarne-Thompson Classification System.* New York: Greenwood Publishing Group, 1987. Mostly adult sources for Aarne-Thompson tale types.

Eastman, Mary Huse. *Index to Fairy Tales, Myths and Legends.* Westwood, Massachusetts: Faxon, 1926.

——————————. *Supplement to Index to Fairy Tales, Myths and Legends.* Westwood, Massachusetts: Faxon, 1937.

_____. *Second Supplement to Index to Fairy Tales, Myths and Legends*. Westwood, Massachusetts: Faxon, 1952.

Ireland, Norma Olin. *Index to Fairy Tales 1973-1977: Including Folklore, Legends, and Myths in Collections*. Westwood, Massachusetts: Faxon, 1985.

_____. *Index to Fairy Tales 1949-1972: Including Folklore, Legends, and Myths in Collections*. Westwood, Massachusetts: Faxon, 1973.

Ireland, Norma Olin and Joseph W. Sprug. *Index to Fairy Tales 1978-1986: Including Folklore, Legends, and Myths in Collections*. Metuchen, New Jersey: Scarecrow Press Inc., 1989.

MacDonald, Margaret Read. "Type and Motif Indexes for Folktale Research." In *Twenty Tellable Tales: Audience Participation Folktales for the Beginning Storyteller*, 199-200. New York: The H.W. Wilson Co., 1986. Listing of scholarly titles.

_____. *The Storyteller's Sourcebook: A Subject, Title, and Motif-Index to Folklore Collections for Children*. Detroit: Neal-Schuman Publishers Inc., 1982. (Second edition prepared by MacDonald and Brian Sturm to be available in 1997.)

Advice on Adapting a Story for Retelling

Barton, Robert. "Making a Story Your Own." In *Tell Me Another: Storytelling and Reading Aloud at Home, at School, and in the Community*, 44-57. Markham, Ontario: Pembroke Publishing Ltd., 1986.

Colwell, Eileen. "Adapting the Story for Telling." In *Storytelling*, 44-52. Westminster College, Oxford: The Thimble Press, 1980. Reprint 1991.

De Wit, Dorothy. "Modifying Tales." In *Children's Faces Looking Up: Program Building for the Storyteller*, 28-54. Chicago: American Library Association, 1979. Gives samples, showing story before and after cutting or expanding.

Griffin, Barbara Budge. "The 'Best Parts' Version." In *Storyteller's Journal: A Guidebook for Story Research and Learning*, 30-32. Medford, Oregon: Barbara Budge Griffin, 10 S. Keeneway Dr., Medford, OR 97504, 1990.

MacDonald, Margaret Read. "Preparing a Tale Text from a Children's Short Story." In *Twenty Tellable Tales: Audience Participation Folktales for the Beginning Storyteller*, 184-85. New York: The H.W. Wilson Co., 1986).

Creating Your Own Story

Cassady, Marsh. *Creating Stories for Storytelling*. San Jose: Resource Publications, 1991.

Moore, Robin. *Awakening the Hidden Storyteller: How to Build a Storytelling Tradition in Your Family*. Boston: Shambhala Publications, Inc., 1991.

Personal Stories

Ross, Ramon Royal. "The Experience Story." In *Storyteller*, 55-71. Columbus: Merrill Publishing Co., 1980.

Steward, Joyce S. and Mary K. Craft. *The Leisure Pen: A Book for Elderwriters*. Plover, Wisconsin: Keepsake Publishers, 1988. Useful for beginning to write personal stories, which you may later tell.

Myths

Cook, Elizabeth. *The Ordinary and the Fabulous: An Introduction to Myths, Legends and Fairy Tales*. Cambridge: Cambridge University Press, c. 1969. Reprint 1976. Sound advice and useful bibliographies for the teller who is ready for the hard work needed to bring myth to life.

Smith, Ron. *Mythologies of the World: A Guide to Sources*. Urbana, Illinois: National Council of Teachers of English, 1981. Detailed bibliographical essays suggesting scholarly sources for the study of mythologies of the world. Use to build your own background in myth.

Defending the Story

We do encourage our children's fantasies; we tell them to paint what they want, or to invent stories. But unfed by our common fantasy heritage, the folk fairy tale, the child cannot invent stories on his own which help him cope with life's problems.

—Bruno Bettelheim, *The Uses of Enchantment*

At times you will face attacks on your story selection. No matter how careful you are, this is apt to happen. Not only are witches and devils taboo in some homes, but fairies and elves are equally abhorred. To comply with the wishes of some parents, we would have to eliminate all literature dealing with fantasy of any sort. Storyteller Bob Polishuk was censored for asking the children to make a wish and blow out a story candle by a parent who considered this act a form of consorting with the supernatural.

In order to respond to parental criticism of your stories you need to find out the basis for their complaints. Some parents are justifiably concerned because of nightmares their children have been enduring. Take this into consideration if you have such a child in your classroom. Realize, however, that to some parents the very act of reading a story about fairies to children puts you in league with the devil. To understand what these parents and their children fear, read *The Seduction of Our Children* by Neil T. Anderson and Steve Russo (Eugene, Oregon: Harvest House, 1991) or *Like Lambs to the Slaughter* by Johanna Michaelsen (Eugene, Oregon: Harvest House, 1989).

Psychologists Defend the Folk/Fairy Tale

Many psychologists defend the frightening effect of fairy tales and insist that children *need* to hear such tales in order to work out their own fears. Without such stories, says Bruno Bettelheim, children believe themselves to be the only ones who imagine such horrors.

> Since what the parent tells him in some strange way happens also to enlighten him about what goes on in the darker and irrational aspects of his mind, this shows the child that he is not alone in his fantasy life, that it is shared by the person he needs and loves most. In such favorable conditions, fairy tales subtly offer suggestions on how to deal constructively with these inner experiences. The fairy story communicates to the child an intuitive, subconscious understanding of his own nature and of what his future may hold if he develops his positive potentials. He senses from fairy tales that to be a human being in this world of ours means having to accept difficult challenges, but also encountering wondrous adventures.[1]

Psychologist Erica Helm Meade suggests that parents whose children have nightmares after hearing scary stories should *thank* the story for bringing this fear to the fore so that it might be dealt with. The tale does not *create* the fear, the tale provides a safe avenue through which the fear can be discussed. She writes:

> As you know, stories convey conscious and unconscious understanding: literal and symbolic meaning. The empathy children feel for struggling heroes and heroines contributes to their emotional education. Stories give youngsters hope that they too can

overcome adversity. Heroes and heroines strive to limit evil. This teaches children about containing their own hostile impulses, and coping with evil in the world. Ethical dilemmas in fairy tales contribute to the child's moral and ethical development. The action and images speak more directly to the young child than abstract explanations. Stories are one of the more gratifying means of learning and contribute greatly to the child's self-esteem.[2]

Read what psychologists have to say about this matter, then prepare your own defense for the materials you will use. Realize that if *you* decide not to tell "Molly Whuppie" because a parent says it frightened her child, it is *you* who are the censor, not the parent who intimidated you.

NOTES

[1] Bruno Bettelheim, *The Uses of Enchantment: The Meaning and Importance of Fairy Tales* (New York: Alfred A. Knopf Inc., 1976), 154-55.

[2] Erica Helm Meade, letter to King County Children's Librarians, June 25, 1992.

BIBLIOGRAPHY

Bettelheim, Bruno. *The Uses of Enchantment: The Meaning and Importance of Fairy Tales.* New York: Alfred A. Knopf Inc., 1976.

Chukovsky, Kornei. "The Battle for the Fairy Tale." In *From Two To Five*, 116-39. Berkeley, California: University of California Press, 1963.

Heuschler, Julius. *A Psychiatric Study of Myths and Fairy Tales: Their Origin, Meaning and Usefulness.* Springfield, Illinois: Charles C. Thomas, Publisher, 1974.

Accepting the Role of Storyteller

What I wanted to do was take what I knew and break it down for those who didn't have the literary teeth to chew it, so they could at least gum it.

I've given my life to storytelling, it's sacred to me. We can touch human hearts forever.

My kind of theater can be presented anywhere, in any setting, with nothin' but a place to stand—and imagination.

—Brother Blue, in *Homespun: Tales from America's Favorite Storytellers*

Folklorists talk of "active" and "passive" tellers. We are all passive tellers. Most of us know the plots of many stories: Cinderella, The Three Bears, Pandora's Box ... but we may never have *told* these stories. Those of you reading this book are about to become *active* tellers. Perhaps you will draw on those tales you already know. Likely you will also select from printed versions tales to bring to life. You will become an active bearer of tradition.

The tales you tell may not come from your own traditional background, but as you retell them for your audiences they *become* a part of your own tradition. Children and other listeners hearing these tales may pick them up and begin retelling them, passing them on, transplanting them from Japan or Ghana to suburban Indianapolis. Of course not all seeds take root, but this is the tradition into which you enter as you become a storyteller.

Accepting the Identity of "Storyteller"

Folklorist Robert J. Adams has written of the "social identity of the storyteller."[1] Perhaps you already identify yourself as a storyteller. Perhaps you are still hesitant to do so. At what point does an individual say, "I am a storyteller"?

Adams studied Japanese teller Tsune Watanabe and came up with a list of the items which contributed to her acceptance of an identity as a storyteller. Let's look at the steps in Mrs. Watanabe's path from story listener to storyteller. Have you passed similar signposts in your story path?

First, Adams says, the potential teller must have a history as a story listener. Possible steps in the individual's path from story listener to storyteller are:

1. The individual listens to stories. As a child Mrs. Watanabe was an avid story listener.

2. The individual identifies with the storyteller. Young Tsune Watanabe identified closely with her mother and her grandfather, both of whom appreciated her desire for stories and told them whenever she asked.

3. The individual instigates storytelling events, seeking out tellers and asking for more stories. Tsune often left her playing to go and ask for stories, while the other children continued at their games.

4. The individual finds that stories contain a reflection of personal beliefs and an expression of personal experiences and values. Adams found that Mrs. Watanabe's tales contained clear representations of her own beliefs, pointed up by asides and by her own tale selection. She projected into the tales her own value system and world view.

5. The individual desires to become a teller. Mrs. Watanabe's desire to please as a teller was so great that she did not rest with the repertoire she had learned from her elders. She read avidly in books from the school library to increase her repertoire.

6. The individual instigates storytelling events in the role of teller. This proved difficult for Mrs. Watanabe since times had changed and her own children were too busy with school and activities to provide a ready audience. She had to plan ahead to arrange storytelling situations for herself. Adams mentions that during his interviews in her home her grandchildren entered and turned on the television, bringing her storytelling to a halt. When Adams appeared with his tape recorder she was thrilled ... an avid listener at last!

Once the desire to become a teller is instilled, there are still factors which must be met if the individual is to assume the identity of "storyteller." Adams suggests that acceptance of the teller by the community depends on:

- the teller's ability to master storytelling techniques;
- the teller's ability to understand and fulfill the needs of the audience; and
- the opportunity to practice telling in a supportive environment.

Think over your own story listening and telling experiences. Have you consciously sought out the role of storyteller?

If you have decided to accept the role, you will be working to master storytelling techniques. You will move toward an understanding of the needs of your audiences. And you will need to begin engineering opportunities to practice your telling—hopefully in a supportive environment!

The way to do this is to let people *know* that you are a teller. Do not be shy about offering your tales. You have a gift to share, but no one will know this unless you make it known. Offer to tell stories for your child's school class, provide a tale for your club's next program, volunteer yourself for the next church potluck as entertainment. If you are a teacher or librarian, use your stories to *barter.* Trade a storytime for something special that another teacher or librarian can provide to your class.

Accept your role of storyteller with pleasure and confidence. This is a special gift that you can share with your family and community.

Giving Yourself Permission to Tell

In this age of increasing cultural exclusiveness I find tellers shying away from folktales which are not ethnically *theirs.* This is a dangerous trend for the life of the folktale. Through the centuries these tales have traveled from culture to culture, passing around the world, changing and growing with each teller. The charming Vietnamese variant of the Cinderella tale is quite different from our French classic. What a loss if the Vietnamese teller had said, "I must not tell this story. It belongs to the French. I was not born to the tale." And think of all the medieval travelers who carried tales and ballads. What if the Spaniard had believed he should never retell a Moroccan tale? And what if the Moroccan had refused to retell anything Spanish?

Our world is as rich as it is because we have shared our stories across cultures, and with them our hopes, our beliefs, our ways of seeing. Now is not the time to freeze all story into pockets of ethnicity. Now more than ever we need each other's stories.

So, after much thought on this matter, I give you a set of assumptions and a set of permissions based on those assumptions. Here then are **MacDonald's Permissions for Storytellers.**

PREMISE: Storytelling is a folk art.
We are the folk.
Storytelling belongs to us.

PREMISE: Storytelling is performance.
Through body language, delivery,

attitude—in every manner—the teller enters a "performing" mode.

PREMISE: Storytelling is more than performance.
It is *event*. Audience and teller interact.
Interaction may become vocal, approaching group drama. Or it may be merely an emotional intensity. The play *between* audience and teller is the heart of the storytelling event.

PREMISE: Storytelling is an audience-shaped art form.
Repeated tellings to sensitive audiences tend to perfect a tale.

PREMISE: There is no one "tale text."
There are only transcriptions of tales taken from one telling of one storyteller. The tale is constantly changing from telling to telling and from teller to teller. There is no *right* text. There are infinite variants.

PREMISE: Each storytelling event has function and meaning within its own cultural context.
Your telling will function within an American cultural context defined by your setting.

Based on these assumptions, let me suggest that you give yourself these permissions:

PERMISSION: It is OK to practice the art of storytelling even if you are not a master teller.

PERMISSION: You don't have to perfect a tale before you begin telling it.
Plunge in and let the audience help mold the story as you tell it. Keep telling and telling until it *does* become perfect.

PERMISSION: It is OK to tell the tales of a culture other than your own. Find out as much as you can about the function of these tales in their own societies. Learn about the context in which the tale was originally told. Share this information with your audience.

PERMISSION: You do not have to tell with ethnic authenticity. It is unlikely that you will be able to do this unless you have roots in the contributing culture. Realize that in your own telling this tale enters the folklore of *your* culture. When I tell a Ghanian folktale to the children in Seattle, Washington, that tale becomes American in function and in the context of its telling. You are *borrowing* from another culture elements which your audience will enjoy. This is *not* cultural reproduction, this is cultural *borrowing*. Be aware of ways in which you are changing the tale and level with your audience about the ways in which your tale has been reworked.

PERMISSION: It is OK to mark the story with your own style. Just relax and do it *your* way. This teller, this tale, this audience create a unique event. You are not replicating. You are *creating*. Feel free to enjoy yourself!

NOTES

[1] Robert J. Adams, *Social Identity of a Japanese Storyteller.* Ph.D. Dissertation, Indiana University, 1972.

BIBLIOGRAPHY

To Celebrate the Storytelling Life Read ...

Sawyer, Ruth. *My Spain: A Storyteller's Year of Collecting.* New York: Viking Press, 1941. Reprint c. 1967.

_____. *The Way of the Storyteller.* New York: Viking Press, 1942. Reprint 1962.

Meet Other Tellers Through ...

Smith, Jimmy Neil. *Homespun: Tales from America's Favorite Storytellers.* New York: Crown Publishing Group, 1988. Brief biographies based on interviews show us how these tellers came to storytelling. One tale from each teller is included.

And Enjoy ...

A Storytelling Calendar. Stinson Beach, California: Stotter Press. Storytelling regalia illustrate the calendar. Each month bears a short tale.

Bibliographies to Help You Explore the World of Storytelling Further

Greene, Ellin and George Shannon. *Storytelling: A Selected Annotated Bibliography.* New York: Garland Publishing Inc., 1986.

Shannon, George W.B. *Folk Literature and Children: An Annotated Bibliography of Secondary Materials.* Westport, Connecticut: Greenwood Publishing Group, 1981.

Networking with Other Tellers

*Something had happened, and even as we sat listening,
we knew we would return the next year and the next.
It was if an ancient memory had been jogged—of
people throughout time, sitting together, hearing
stories: a congregation of listeners. We were taken
back to a time when the story, transmitted orally, was
all there was. How had we wandered so far from the
oral tradition? What had pulled us away?*

—Jimmy Neil Smith, *Homespun: Tales from America's Favorite Storytellers*

*It seems like whenever stories and storytellers are
together, there's a little magic ... a little magic that
happens.*

—Jay Stailey, NAPPS Board Retreat, 1993

You may wish to join hands with other tellers in some of
the support groups available today. Here is information to
help you connect.

The National Association for the Preservation and Perpetuation of Storytelling (NAPPS)

NAPPS, with headquarters in Jonesborough, Tennessee,
serves as a connecting point for many tellers. The organization publishes a quarterly journal, *Storytelling Magazine,* a bi-
monthly newsletter, *The Yarnspinner,* an annual catalog of

storytelling resources, and the *National Directory of Story-telling,* an annual listing of professional storytellers, storytelling conferences, and storytelling organizations.

NAPPS also sponsors an annual conference, held at a different location each year, and the National Storytelling Festival, held each October in Jonesborough. Under the strong leadership of its executive director, Jimmy Neil Smith, NAPPS makes good use of the media and fosters a strong commitment to the tradition of storytelling. Its headquarters houses an archive of storytelling resources featuring audio and video tapes. NAPPS has more than seven thousand members, including most professional tellers and many educators and librarians, as well as ministers and psychologists who use story. And of course many members are just plain story lovers.

Regional and Local Storytelling Guilds

NAPPS is associated through mutual endeavours with regional storytelling organizations such as the Northlands Storytelling Network, the Tejas Storytelling Association, the League for the Advancement of New England Storytelling (LANES), and with local groups such as the Seattle Storyteller's Guild and the Sacramento Storyteller's Guild. For a listing of storytelling associations in your area see the *National Directory of Story-telling,* available from NAPPS.

Each year, on the last Thursday in November, many of these organizations join in sponsoring a Tellabration, a night of storytelling which is held simultaneously in more than one hundred locations throughout the U.S., Canada, and overseas.

Beginning tellers will profit from joining a local storytelling organization. A membership with NAPPS will keep you abreast of storytelling trends. Many new tellers find this connection exciting and useful.

The National Story League

The National Story League, founded in 1903, offers workshops, conferences, and local support groups. Its motto is "Service through Storytelling"; members give their services free of charge in schools, churches, hospitals, and nursing homes. The organization's purpose is "to encourage the appreciation of the good and beautiful in life and literature through the art of storytelling." The National Story League has more than one thousand members and is divided into three districts, with local leagues. Tellers interested in providing storytelling as a community service will find support from these story leagues. The organization publishes a quarterly magazine, *Story Art.*

FOR MORE INFORMATION

NAPPS
P.O. Box 309
Jonesborough, TN 37659
Phone: 800-525-4514

The National Story League
c/o Miss Marion O. Kiligas
259 E. 41st Street
Norfolk, VA 23504

Why Tell?
Examining the Values
of Storytelling

When the legends die, the dreams end. When
the dreams end, there is no more greatness.

—Hal Borland, *When the Legends Die*

Why invest time and energy to learn and tell stories?
Here are a few things story can do.

For the Individual

1. Hearing and telling tales hones our literary and imaginative skills. We improve our ability to:

- Listen
- Speak
- Imagine
- Compose phrases
- Create story

2. Sharing story broadens our awareness of other cultures and gives us a deeper understanding of our own. We begin to understand some of the many ways of being.

3. Through story we begin to understand ourselves. Story helps us see, helps us verbalize, points up hidden messages from our lives.

4. Story listening gives us a sense of belonging in a group, it gives us a sense of being nurtured by the teller.

5. Story allows us a quiet space in which to think, and an emotional release in which gasping, laughing, or crying are *expected* behaviors.

For the Group

6. Story bonds a group together. The story becomes a shared experience. Sharing the story's joy or grief bonds us.

For the Community

7. Story can pass on morals, values, beliefs. It can seek to regulate behavior.

8. Story can be used to preserve traditions, to pass on history.

For the Teller

9. Story carries the ability to calm a group—or to energize them. Story offers you the power to hold a group in your sway.

10. Story can give you the pride of performance and the joy of sharing.

Each teller should prepare a personal list of reasons for telling. Know why *you* tell. If you are a teacher, keep on hand a typed list of learning objectives filled by your storytelling activities. This will remind you that telling *is* teaching.

Dr. Spencer Shaw provides a list of the values of storytime for young children:

> Free for the moment from questioning adults, and emotionally and mentally liberated, each child may discover many things when books are shared:
> *Happiness*: to release uninhibited laughter and rhythmic responses of small bodies.
> *Wonder*: to foster fresh, childlike speculations as the stories unfold.

Self-discovery: to permit visual and
mental explorations far removed from
reality.

Quiet solitude: to offer a retreat from
the frenetic pace of seemingly endless
activities.

Companionship: to be found in a group
experience or in having shared identity
with a fictional counterpart or with a
storyteller who does not acknowledge any
disparity between ages.

Budding understanding: to excite
young minds to stretch into the unknown
and the new.

Creativity: to encourage little tongues to
try out unfamiliar words, little hands to
mold symbolic images into objective
realities.[1]

In *Look What Happened to Frog: Storytelling in Education*, Pamela J. Cooper and Rives Collins suggest these values: storytelling enhances imagination and visualization; teaches an appreciation of the beauty and rhythm of language; increases vocabulary; enhances speaking and listening skills; allows students to interact with adults on a personal level; enhances writing, reading skills, and critical- and creative-thinking skills; nourishes students' intuitive side; helps students realize the importance of literature as a mirror of human experience; helps students understand their cultural heritage and those of others.[2]

In *Storytelling for Young Adults*, Gail De Vos discusses telling stories to young adults as an aid in search for identity; in developing value systems; in establishing a sense of belonging; in individual contemplation; to encourage emotional release; in developing imagination; in entertaining; in the creation of bonds; in developing listening skills; in preserving traditions; in remembering cultural stories; in exposing young adults to oral language; and in developing literary discrimination.[3]

Perhaps most importantly, story offers the power to bind us together and heal our wounds. Here are the words of Rex Ellis, from his opening remarks as chairperson of the board of the National Association for the Preservation and Perpetuation of Storytelling (NAPPS):

> I truly believe that the power of storytelling is the one best hope we have to improve the communities we live in and the people we love.... I have seen people with different backgrounds talk to each other for the first time. I have seen fathers, mothers, and sons and daughters who seldom speak to each other laughing, reminiscing, and reconnecting because of storytelling. I have seen inner-city kids who have decided to leave their guns at home and express the stories they so desperately need to tell with pencils and paper instead. I have seen bridges built with storytelling that invite listeners and tellers to unite in ways that are more potent than a town meeting and more healing than a therapy session. It is pretty hard to hate someone whose story you know.[2]

NOTES

[1] Spencer G. Shaw, "First Steps: Storytime with Young Listeners," in *Start Early for an Early Start: You and the Young Child* (Chicago: American Library Association, 1976), 41-42.

[2] Pamela J. Cooper and Rives Collins, *Look What Happened to Frog: Storytelling in Education* (Scottsdale, Arizona: Gorsuch Scarisbrick Publishers, 1992), 11-20.

[3] Gail De Vos, *Storytelling for Young Adults: Techniques and Treasury* (Littleton, Colorado: Libraries Unlimited, 1991), 2-7.

[4] Rex Ellis, Chairperson of the Board, National Association for the Preservation and Perpetuation of Storytelling board meeting, February 1993.

Belonging to the Story

*We want to internalize the story, like a musician who
has played "My Funny Valentine" a zillion times. And
when the story is internalized, we're on automatic.
Now we're free to give the story power—to give
ourselves over to the tale and the tellin'.*

—Brother Blue, in *Homespun: Tales from
America's Favorite Storytellers*

I have developed my technique for learning a story in one
hour in the hopes of pushing onlookers into the stream of
storytelling. Most will find that story *is* fun, that they *can*
keep afloat on their story. I am counting on getting these new
tellers hooked on story. But there is a danger in my technique.
The danger is that this method may breed tellers who imagine
storytelling to be so simple that it needs no work. Learn a
quick story, toss it off, go on to the next.

Yet to truly *belong* to a story, you must tell it many times.
You must share it with many audiences, and always you must
critique yourself and grow with your story. Ruth Sawyer offers excellent advice:

> Traditional storytellers had vital pride in
> what they had to tell, a deep sense of be-
> longing. Back to me ran the voices of half a
> dozen I had listened to: "Here's a tale that
> will bide long with ye. 'Tis proud I am to
> tell it" ... "Did ye ever hear about Rory, the
> robber? I had the tale from my grandad, and
> he from his" ... "Hearken to this one. 'Tis
> about Hughie, the smith of Inver. 'Tis as
> gentle a tale as ye'll be after hearing." Pride

in the telling, a strong sense of kinship with everything they had to tell, an easy, effortless flowing of words. And still there was something I lacked—an established friendliness with the listeners, and a kind of jubilation at the sharing of it.[1]

As a children's librarian I always consider that I have two responsibilities. One is to the child—to find the right book for him or her; the other is the gift I owe the *book*—to find for it the right reader. So it is with our tales. There are listeners waiting who need certain tales. There are tales which need to find their proper listeners. When you have told your tale over and over, when you have learned to love it and its telling, when you finally belong to the story ... then you can use it as it needs to be used.

NOTES

[1] Ruth Sawyer, *The Way of the Storyteller* (New York: Viking Press, 1942), 86-87.

Stories Audiences Have Loved

Here are twelve stories my audiences have enjoyed. All encourage audience participation. All feature enough repetition to make them easy to remember. All encourage energetic, playful responses in both teller and audience. Children *and* adults who aren't afraid to let themselves play will love these. These tales are not to be *performed* before an audience; they are designed for group play. *You* know the story. You will lead the playing. But your audience will own the story with you. This is their event.

Turtle of Koka. Easiest of all. Very simple repetition. Your audience will teach you to relax and play with story if you tell them this one. *All ages, but especially grades K-5.*

The Little Old Woman Who Lived in a Vinegar Bottle. Easy-to-learn repetition. A bit precious for some. *Preschool, primary grades.*

Puchika Churika. Repetition makes it easy to learn. *Preschool, primary grades.*

Marsh Hawk. Spunky, colloquial. *Preschool-Grade 5.*

Gecko. Active. Audience can add in characters, giving this an improvisational quality. Praises persistence. Very popular with my audiences. *Grades K-5.*

Kudu Break! You can use audience members to act out parts of this. Children will ask to play it again. One of my most frequently requested tales. *Grades K-6.*

What Are Their Names! Complicated rhythmic fun. *Grades K-5.*

Aayoga with Many Excuses. Clear structure on which to hang dialogue. Children like the imagery. Pointed message. *Preschool-Grade 4.*

Kanu Above and Kanu Below. More lengthy than others in this book, but well worth the effort. A kind, healing message. *Ages K-adult.*

Ko Kóngole. Energetic, rhythmic chant. Great fun for groups. *All ages.*

Ningun. Delightfully creepy tale of a girl who follows a forbidden lover. And is eaten by a boa. One inch at a time. You must *love* it to tell it. Lots of chanting and munching. *Grade 4-adult, younger if they aren't easily terrified.*

Yonjwa Seeks a Bride. Hard-hitting courtship story. *Strength* is prized in a bride. Tell it with spunk and humor. *Grade 5-adult (good junior-high, teen story).*

Accompanying each tale are hints for performing the tale, along with notes discussing key motifs in the tale and referring to other variants of this tale in world folklore. The tale notes will use "Motif" and "Type" numbers to discuss the tales. Folklorists assign numbers to folktales much like librarians assign Dewey Decimal numbers to books.

For example, Cinderella is Type 510. Each building block of the folktale is given a separate motif number. Cinderella includes motifs such as C761.4 *Staying too long at the ball*; H36.1 *Slipper test*; and R221 *Threefold flight from the ball*. This helps us recognize the many variations of a tale when they appear in the folk literature of many countries in many languages.

In these tale notes I refer repeatedly to three folktale indexes: *The Storyteller's Sourcebook: A Subject, Title, and Motif-Index to Folklore Collections for Children* by Margaret Read MacDonald (Detroit: Neal-Schuman / Gale Research, 1982), the *Motif-Index of Folk-Literature* by Stith Thompson (Bloomington: Indiana University, 1966), and *The Types of the Folktale* by Antti Aarne and Stith Thompson (Helsinki: Folklore Fellows Communication, 1961). Of these, *The Storyteller's Sourcebook*, which incorporates Thompson's numbering system is the one you will want to become familiar with and use. The other two are scholarly indexes available in university collections. However, since *all* folktale indexing is based on those two indexes, you should know that they exist.

Turtle of Koka

Let me tell you about Turtle of Koka.
A man of Lubi la Suku caught a turtle.
He brought it to the village.
>   "Let's make turtle stew!"
>   "But how shall we kill it?"

Someone said:
"Let's use our hatchet."
Turtle of Koka was so brave.
He jumped up on his little hind legs and began to dance and
>   brag before them all.

He was telling them they could not hurt *him* with a hatchet.
>   "Turtle of Koka
>   Turtle of Koka
>   Hard hard shell!
>   Hard hard shell!
>   Hatchet of Koka
>   Hatchet of Koka
>   Can't hurt *me*.
>   Can't hurt *me!*"

Now you know that the hatchet really would hurt Turtle.
But he fooled those people with his bluffing.
>   "Then how can we kill this turtle?"
>   "Maybe with a knife?"

But Turtle jumped up and began to dance and sing again.
>   "Turtle of Koka
>   Turtle of Koka
>   Hard hard shell!
>   Hard hard shell!
>   Knife of koka
>   Knife of koka
>   Can't hurt *me*
>   Can't hurt *me!*"

>   "A knife won't hurt him either.

THE STORYTELLER'S START-UP BOOK

What can we use?"

"Maybe a big stick?"

Up jumped Turtle and began to sing.
> "Turtle of Koka
> Turtle of Koka
> Hard hard shell!
> Hard hard shell!
> Big stick of Koka
> Big stick of Koka
> Can't hurt *me*
> Can't hurt *me!*"

The people tried first one thing and then another.
Turtle kept singing his mocking song.
They believed his bluffing.

At last someone said
> "What if we threw him into the water?
> Then he would drown and we could eat him."

When Turtle of Koka heard that he pretended to be *very*
   frightened.
He began to tremble all over and cry.
> "Water of Koka ...
> water of Koka ...
> no ... no ... no ...
> no ... no ... no ...
> Water of Koka ...
> Water of Koka ...
> no ... no ... no ...
> no ... no ... no ..."

"That is the thing to do!" said the people.
"That is the thing this Turtle of Koka is *afraid* of.
We will *drown* him!"

Now you and I know that Turtle *lives* in the water.
Water can't hurt Turtle at all.
But he had fooled those people.

They took that turtle to the river.
They *threw* him in.
Turtle sank out of sight into the river.

The people waited for Turtle to drown and float to the top of
    the water.

But water was Turtle's home.

Turtle swam to the top of the water.
He stuck out his little head.
He laughed and sang.
     "Water of Koka
     Water of Koka
     That's my *home!*
     That's my *home!*
     Water of Koka
     Water of Koka
     Bye ... bye ... bye ...
     Bye ... bye ... bye ..."

Then he dove under the water and swam away.
And no one saw Turtle of Koka again.

Tips for Telling

    This is such a simple story that you can learn it quickly. The story can be told in a straightforward way, relating Turtle's responses to hatchet, stick, and other implements you may choose to add. Stretch the tale as long as you like by simply adding choruses as the villagers try to break him open with a sword, axe, sledgehammer, etc. This sounds a little brutal, but it is a humorous story when told, as Turtle's spunky song outwits them all.

THE STORYTELLER'S START-UP BOOK

To have even more fun with this tale, let your audience suggest ways to break open Turtle's shell: "What do *you* think they should try?" I pick one of the waving hands, and the child suggests, "Try a hammer!"

"Do you think a hammer would hurt *me?*" I let Turtle say to the child. "My shell is *too* hard!" And he launches into his song again.

This group play can go on as long as you like. Don't be surprised if you end up with bazookas and hand grenades, with Turtle still insisting his shell is too hard to crack.

Because the story can be expanded indefinitely, this tale makes a useful ending when you are presenting an entire program of stories and your sponsor expects you to end the performance at exactly 2:05.

When Turtle sings, I show him dancing around and patting himself on the back as he calls "Hard hard shell" and "Can't hurt *me!*" I sometimes mime the chopping action of a hatchet, sword, etc. as he sings of the proposed weapon. This story calls for a free spirit and a willingness to relax and play with your audience. It is such a simple story that you can hardly go wrong with it, so it is a good place to begin dabbling with improvisational telling.

About the Story

"Turtle of Koka" is elaborated from a brief tale in *Folk-Tales of Angola: Fifty Tales, with Ki-Mbundu Text* by Heli Chatelain (Boston and New York: Published for the American Folk-Lore Society by G.E. Stechert & Co., 1894, pp. 153-155). Here is a sample Ki-Mbundu text for turtle's chant:

Mbaxi a Koka	Turtle of Koka
Ni Kua a Koka	And hatchet of Koka
Dikda k-a ngi di kama	Hatchet not kills me a bit.

Chatelain explains that the word *koka* is a pun in the story because it has extended meanings. *Koka* means "to drag," and so a turtle, who drags along the ground, is a "turtle of koka"; but it also means "to cut down a tree," so a hatchet is a "hatchet of koka"; by extension a stone, which is as hard as a turtle's shell, is named "koka," after the turtle. Audiences usually think *koka* means "hard." This seems close enough to the truth of the tale.

Chatelain explains that the small turtle of the Malaji Plateau, about whom this story is told, lives as much on land as in the water, which explains why Turtle's ruse works.

This story is an example of Motif K581.1 *Drowning punishment for turtle (eel, crab). By expressing horror of drowning, he induces his captor to throw him into the water—his home* and of Type 1310 *Drowning the Crayfish as Punishment. Eel, crab, turtle, etc. express fear of water and are thrown in.* This popular folktale motif is found in the Indian Jatakas and throughout the world. *The Storyteller's Sourcebook* lists many sources: African-American, Angola, Ceylon, Cherokee, East Africa, Haiti, Hopi, India (Jataka), Philippines, Poland, West India. Stith Thompson's *Motif-Index of Folk-Literature* adds sources from England, Denmark, Indonesia, Nigeria, and Zanzibar. *The Types of the Folktale* by Antti Aarne and Stith Thompson cites in addition sources from twelve European countries, Argentina, Cuba, the Dominican Republic, and Puerto Rico.

The Little Old Woman Who Lived in a Vinegar Bottle

There once was a little old woman who lived in a *vinegar bottle.*
Don't ask me why.
It was a common old vinegar bottle.
But unusually large, of course.
Still it did make a very cramped house.

Every day the old woman would sit on her front step and complain about her house.
> "Oh what a pity!
> What a pity pity pity!
> That I should have to live in a house such as this.
> Why, *I* should be living in a dear little cottage with a thatched roof.
> And roses growing up the walls."

Just then a fairy happened to be passing by.
When she heard the old woman she thought,
> "Well, if that's what she wants ...
> that's what she'll *get."*

And going up to the old woman she said,
> "When you go to bed tonight
> turn round three times
> and close your eyes.
> When you open them in the morning
> see what you shall see."

Well the old woman thought the fairy was likely batty.
But when she went to bed that night
> she turned round three times
> and closed her eyes.

In the morning when she opened them again ...
She was in a dear little cottage!
With a thatched roof
and roses growing up the walls.

"It's just what I've always wanted," she said.
"How content I'll be living *here*."
But she said not a word of thanks to the fairy.

Well the fairy went north
and the fairy went south.
The fairy went east
and the fairy went west.
She did all the business she had to do.

Then the fairy remembered the old woman.
    "I wonder how she's getting on in her cottage.
    She must be very happy indeed.
    I'll just stop by for a visit."

But when the fairy came near,
she saw the old woman sitting on her front step ...
    complaining.
    "Oh what a pity!
    What a pity pity pity!
    That I should have to live in a cramped little cottage
        like this.
    Why I should be living in a fine row house.
    With handsome houses on either side
    and lace curtains at the window
    and a brass knocker on the door!"

    "I can do that," thought the fairy.
    "If that's what she wants ...
    that's what she'll *get*."
And to the old woman she said,
    "When you go to bed tonight
    turn round three times

and close your eyes.
When you open them in the morning
see what you see."

The old woman didn't have to be told twice.
She went right to bed.
She turned round three times
and closed her eyes.
In the morning when she opened them ...
she was in a spanking new *row* house!
With neighbors on either side
and lace curtains at the window
and a brass knocker on the door.

"It's just what I always *wanted,*" said the old woman.
"I'll be so contented *here.*"
But she never said a word of thanks to the fairy.

The fairy went north
and the fairy went south.
The fairy went east
and the fairy went west.
She did all the business she had to do.

Then she thought about the old woman.
    "I wonder how that old woman is doing these days?
    The one that used to live in the *vinegar bottle.*
    I'll just stop round and see."
But when she came to the old woman's fine house,
the old woman was sitting in her shiny new rocking chair,
rocking and ... *complaining.*
    "Oh what a pity!
    What a pity pity pity!
    That I should have to live in a row house like this.
    With common folk on either side.
    I should live in a mansion on the hill.
    With a maidservant and a manservant to do my
        bidding.

That's what *I* deserve."

When the fairy heard that she was much amazed.
But she said,
>"Well, if that's what she wants ...
>that's what she'll *get.*"

And to the old woman she said,
>"When you go to bed tonight
>turn round three times
>and close your eyes.
>And when you open them in the morning
>see what you shall see."

So the old woman hopped into bed.
She turned round three times.
She closed her eyes.
And in the morning when she opened them again ...
she was in a mansion on the hill!
With a maidservant and a manservant to do her bidding.

"This is just what I've always *wanted,*" said the old woman.
"How contented I will be *here.*"
But it never occurred to her to thank the fairy.

Well the fairy went north
and the fairy went south.
The fairy went east
and the fairy went west.
She did all the business she had to do.

Then she remembered the old woman again.
>"I wonder how that old woman is getting on now.
>The old woman who used to live in a *vinegar bottle.*
>She must be quite happy in her new mansion."

But when she came near, she saw the old woman
sitting in her velvet chair ... *complaining.*

"Oh what a pity!
What a pity pity pity!
That I should have to live all alone in this old
      mansion.
Why *I* should be the *queen.*
I should be living in the *palace.*
With ladies in waiting for company
and musicians to entertain me.
That's what *I* deserve."

"Good heavens," thought the fairy.
"Will she *never* be content?
Well, if that's what she wants ...
that's what she'll *get."*

To the old woman she said,
      "When you go to bed tonight
      turn round three times
      and close your eyes.
      And in the morning
      see what you shall see."

The old woman hurried to bed.
She turned round three times.
She closed her eyes.
In the morning ...
She was in the *palace!*
With ladies in waiting to keep her company
and musicians to entertain her."

This is what I've always wanted," said the old woman.
"I will be very contented living *here."*
But she forgot entirely to thank the fairy.

The fairy went north
and the fairy went south.
The fairy went east
and the fairy went west.

She did all the business she had to do.

Then she began to wonder about that old woman again.
"I wonder how that old woman is getting along ...
The old woman who used to live in a *vinegar bottle.*"

So she stopped at the palace to see.
There sat the old woman on her throne
and she was ... *complaining!*
>"Oh what a pity!
>What a pity pity pity!
>That I should be queen of such a tiny little kingdom.
>Why I should be the Pope in Rome.
>The Pope rules the Holy Roman Empire.
>Then I could rule the minds of *everybody* in the
>   world!
>That's what *I* deserve."

"Well!" said the fairy.
"If *that's* what she wants ...
that's what she'll *not* get!"

And to the old woman she said,
>"When you go to bed tonight
>turn around three times
>and close your eyes.
>And in the morning
>*see what you shall see.*"

The old woman went right to bed.
She turned round three times.
She closed her eyes.
And in the morning when she opened them ...
she was *right back in her vinegar bottle!*

"And there she shall stay," said the fairy.
"If she's not content here
she won't be content *there.*"

After all, contentment comes from the *heart,*
not from the *house.*

Tips for Telling

Children love the repetition of this tale. They will soon repeat with you the second half of the fairy's retort: "Well, if that's what she wants ... that's what she'll *get!*"

The little old woman should be very whiny, of course. Don't worry too much about getting her house descriptions just as I have them. As long as she keeps moving up in the world, you can give her any sort of mansion you like. I try to keep to the houses in Briggs's source since I like the British flavor there. Be sure to keep the fairy's north / south / east / west bit, though. It is rhythmic and makes a pleasing respite within the story.

About the Story

This is a variant of Motif B375.1 *Fish returned to water: grateful* and Type 555 *The Fisher and His Wife.* The best-known version is that of the Brothers Grimm, in which a fish grants a wish to a man whose wife demands that he wish for ever greater homes. In the British version, the wish is granted directly to the old woman herself, who lives in a vinegar bottle. She is usually granted the wish by a fish, but in a delightful variant given by Katherine M. Briggs in *A Dictionary of British Folk-Tales* (Bloomington: Indiana University Press, 1970, V.l, pp. 437-439) the wish is given by a busy little fairy. Briggs lists the story as a "Camp-fire story, 1924," with no teller given. This seems an especially well-developed version of the tale, with the fairy's rhythmic gadding about and the old woman rolling round three times in her bed.

For another interesting British variant see Rumer Godden's *Old Woman Who Lived in a Vinegar Bottle* (New York:

Viking Press, 1970). Hers is a quite elaborate version, which she says was passed down in her family.

Though the Grimms' version is best known in the United States, *The Types of the Folktale* by Antti Aarne and Stith Thompson cites variants from twenty-six European countries, Indonesia, the Caribbean (thirteen sources) and Africa (eleven sources). See Motif B375.1 in *The Storyteller's Sourcebook* by Margaret Read MacDonald for many variants available in children's books.

Puchika Churika

Little Puchika Churika lived with his Momma and his Poppa
and his Big Brother in a tent on the tundra.

One day Puchika Churika's Momma and Poppa and Big
Brother all went out to hunt for food.
Little Puchika Churika had to stay behind, all alone, in the
big empty tent.
His Momma said,
"Puchika Churika, here is a pot of porridge for your
lunch.
And here is a big spoon to eat it with.
Now, Puchika Churika, while we are gone ...
do *not* go outside the tent.
Puchika Churika, while we are gone ...
behave yourself.
And they left.

While they were gone,
Puchika Churika did *not* go outside the tent.
But *did* he behave himself?
We shall see.

With Momma and Poppa and Big Brother gone,
Puchika Churika was bored.
First he played string figures to entertain himself.
He was still bored.
So he told himself stories.
He was still bored.
He ate his porridge with his big porridge spoon.
Then he put down his spoon and said
"Thanks for the porridge, spoon.
Here is a bite of porridge for *you.*"
And he said to the porridge pot.
"Thanks for the porridge, pot.

Here is a bite of porridge for *you.*"
Then he was bored again.

Puchika Churika took out his little knife and began to *carve*
on the *tent pole.*
He should *not* have done *that.*
First he carved his *name.*
"P ... U ... C ... H ... I ... K ... A ...
C ... H ... U ... R ... I ... K ... A."
Then he began to carve a picture of a deer.
It was a good enough picture of a deer ...
but it *shouldn't* be carved on a *tent pole.*

Suddenly Puchika Churika heard a whuffling noise outside
the tent flap.
A voice called.
"Puchika Churika ... are you inside?"
It was *Old Man Whiskers!*
"Not Old Man Whiskers!!!"
Puchika Churika knew better than to answer.
He kept *very* quiet.

Old Man Whiskers tried something else.
"Is little Puchika Churika's Momma home today?
I've come to see little Puchika Churika's Momma."

"Oh no, she's not home," said Puchika Churika.
"She's out trapping for fish."

"Then I'll go find her and give her such a *scare!*" growled
Old Man Whiskers.

"You'd better not *try* it," said Puchika Churika.
"My Momma has a big fish knife.
And she will chop you in half.
And half will fly up to the sky.
And half will sink down into the ground!"

"Ooooohhh.
Then I won't go scare Puchika Churika's Momma.
Is Puchika Churika's Poppa at home?
I've come to see Puchika Churika's Poppa."
"No, he is out hunting black fowl."

"Then I'll go find him and give him such a *scare!*"

"You'd better not do *that!*
Puchika Churika's Poppa has a big *axe.*
He will chop you in half.
And half will fly up to the sky.
And half will sink down into the ground!"

"Oooohhh.
Then I won't go scare Puchika Churika's Poppa.
Is Puchika Churika's Big Brother at home?"

"No. He's out hunting grey fowl."

"Then I will go find him and give him such a scare!"

"Don't do *that!*
Puchika Churika's Big Brother has a knife even bigger than
        his Momma's.
He will chop you in half.
And half will fly up to the sky.
And half will sink down to the ground."

"Oooohh ...
Then I won't go scare Puchika Churika's Big Brother.
But if Puchika Churika's Momma ...
and his Poppa ...
and his Big Brother ...
are all out hunting food ...
then little Puchika Churika must be home *alone!*"

Puchika Churika had given himself away!

He ran quick and hid under a pile of skins in the corner.

Old Man Whiskers *lifted* the tent flap.
Old Man Whiskers began to *snoop* around the tent.
"Do *you* know where Puchika Churika is hiding?"
He asked every thing in the tent.
He kicked the porridge pot.
"Do *you* know where Puchika Churika is hiding?"

"Puchika Churika gives me a bite of everything he tastes,"
    said the porridge pot.
"I won't tell where he is hiding."

Old Man Whiskers kicked the porridge spoon.
"Do *you* know where Puchika Churika is hiding?"

"Puchika Churika gives me a bite of everything he tastes,"
    said the porridge spoon.
"I won't tell where he is hiding."

Old Man Whiskers kicked the tent post.
"Do *you* know where Puchika Churika is hiding?"

"Puchika Churika carved into my back all afternoon," said
    the tent post.
"And he really hurt me too!
I'll tell you where he is hiding.
Right there under those skins!"

Old Man Whiskers whisked off those skins.
Old Man Whiskers *gobbled* Puchika Churika down in one
    gulp!

Puchika Churika was *so* indignant.
He was stuck inside Old Man Whiskers' icky stomach!
He took out his little knife and began to poke on Old Man
    Whiskers' stomach.
"Poke ... poke ... poke ... poke ..."

What a tummyache that gave Old Man Whiskers!
"Oh ... this little Puchika Churika is giving me a *tummy ache!*
Puchika Churika is making my stomach *hurt!*"

Then Puchika Churika carved himself a little door and
hopped right out of Old Man Whiskers' stomach.
With a roar, Old Man Whiskers grabbed his tummy and ran
out of the tent and away over the tundra.

Soon Puchika Churika's Momma and Poppa and Big Brother
came home.
"Puchika Churika, come out!" called his Momma.
"Come out and help carry in the fish!"

"I *can't* come out," cried Puchika Churika.
"I was stuck inside Old Man Whiskers' stomach.
I am all *yucky!*"

"Puchika Churika, come out!" called his Poppa.
"Come out and help carry in the black fowl."
"I *can't* come out," cried Puchika Churika.
"I was stuck inside Old Man Whiskers' stomach.
I am all *yucky!*"

"Puchika Churika, come out!" called his Big Brother.
"Come out and help me carry in the grey fowl."
"I *can't* come out," cried Puchika Churika.
"I was stuck inside Old Man Whiskers' stomach.
I am all *yucky!*"

His Momma and his Poppa and his Big Brother ran into the
tent.
There was little Puchika Churika.
He was all *yucky!*

"Quick, boil some water!" said Puchika Churika's Momma.
She washed him from top to bottom.

And then she washed his clothes and dried them.
And when she had dressed Puchika Churika again,
he was as good as ever.

"Thank you Porridge Pot, for not telling where I was
    hiding," said Puchika Churika.
"Thank you Porridge Spoon, for not telling where I was
    hiding."
"No thanks to *you,* tent pole, for *telling* on me."

"No thanks to *you,* Puchika Churika, for carving on my
    back."

        "I'm sorry," said Puchika Churika.
        "I won't do it again."
        And he didn't.

As for Old Man Whiskers,
he *never* came back.
If *you* had eaten something that gave you *such a
    tummyache,*
would you come back for *more?*
I think *not.*

Tips for Telling

This story is a bit precious in tone, and I'm not sure I approve of Puchika Churika's gory threats, but children from kindergarten to second grade adore this story. They like the spunky way little Puchika Churika stands up to Old Man Whiskers, understand why the tent poles turn him in, and are comforted when Momma washes and dries little Puchika Churika at the tale's end.

I changed the "Old Man the Devil" of the original to "Old Man Whiskers" since our culture has specific connotations for "devil" which probably were not intended in the Siberian original. Children often see Old Man Whiskers as a huge bear or other animal. This seems fine; he is the prototypical ogre, after all.

About the Story

This tale was inspired by "Puchika-Churika," a Selkup tale included in *Northern Lights: Fairy Tales of the Peoples of the North* compiled by E. Pomerantseva and translated by Irina Zheleznova (Progress Publishers, 1976), pp. 124-126. My "Old Man Whiskers" is referred to as "Old Man the Devil" in this version.

This story hinges on Motif F912 *Victim kills swallower from within*. This motif is found around the world. Mac-Donald's *Storyteller's Sourcebook* cites many sources: Zulu, Bantu, Eskimo, Haida, Sioux, Chippewa, Haitian, Nez Perce, Mexican, Cheyenne, Korean, Choco (South America), Finnish, German, Baganda, Spanish, African-American, and Congolese.

In the Norwegian tale of "Little Buttercup," the child responds to the witch's questions about his family with a similar dialogue. For a variant of that story see Margaret Read MacDonald, *When the Lights Go Out: Twenty Scary Tales to Tell* (New York: The H.W. Wilson Co., 1986), pp. 7-20.

Marsh Hawk

Marsh Hawk flew here.
Marsh Hawk flew there.
Marsh Hawk was so hungry.
He was looking for something good to eat.
Marsh Hawk flew over Chipmunk Village.
There were the little chipmunks.
They were running around with their tails in the air.
They were scampering in and out of their hole.
They were sitting up on their little haunches and chipping ...
      "Chee ... chee ... chee ... chee ... chee ..."

Marsh Hawk perched on a tall fir tree.
He called down to those little chipmunks.
      "Hey you guys!
      Do you have *fat fat* little tummies?
      I bet you've got *fat fat* little tummies, for sure."
The chipmunks giggled.
      "Yes, we have *fat fat* little tummies.
      Sure we do."
Marsh Hawk said to himself, "I'm going to *eat* those fat fat
    little tummies!"
He spread his wings and soared down.
The chipmunks saw his shadow.
They *scampered* right into their hole!
Marsh Hawk didn't catch even one.

He peered into their hole.
They were in there ... all huddled in the back.
Marsh Hawk *reached* in with his claw.
He couldn't reach them.
Marsh Hawk *reached* in with his wing.
He couldn't reach them.
Marsh Hawk *reached* in with his beak.
He couldn't reach them.

"Hey you guys.
You still got those fat fat little tummies?"

"Sure, you betcha.
We still have fat fat little tummies."

"Come out here and let me see your fat fat little
    tummies."

"Oh no.
We don't want to come out there and let you see our
    fat fat little tummies."

"Please come out and let me see your fat fat little
    tummies."

"Well ... would you *dance* for us?
If you dance for us,
we'll come out."

"Sure, I can dance."
Marsh Hawk went to the middle of the meadow.
He began to dance.
    "Uwi ha hi
    Uwi ha hi
    Chipmunks come out and look at me-ee!"

He was dancing around all over the place.
He threw his head back.
He closed his eyes.
He was dancing and dancing ...
turning around and around.

Those little chipmunks crept out very quietly.
First one ... then another ...
        scamper ... scamper ... scamper ...
Soon they had all run out of that hole and away.

"Funny I don't hear them chattering anymore ...
     Hunh?"
Marsh Hawk looked around.
No chipmunks.
He looked into their hole.
No chipmunks.
     "You guys!
     you *tricked* me!
     I'm going away now.
     But I'll be back.
     I'll catch you all.
     You with your fat fat little tummies."
Marsh Hawk flew away.

The chipmunks came out and began to play again in the
    meadow.
Some ran around with their tails in the air.
Some ran in and out of their hole.
Some sat up on their haunches and chattered.
     "Chee ... chee ... chee ... chee ..."

Marsh Hawk flew back.
He perched on that tall fir tree.
     "I'll sing a song.
     I'll make those chipmunks stick up their tails.
     Then I'll fly down there and grab their tails in my
        beak and carry off a whole bunch of them!"
Marsh Hawk began to sing:
     "Uwi ha hi
     Uwi ha hi
     Chipmunks stick your tails in the air!"

He sang and sang.
Those chipmunks all stuck their tails up in the air.
They looked around.
Marsh Hawk swooped down.
The chipmunks saw his shadow and *scampered!*
Right into their hole!

Marsh Hawk didn't catch a single chipmunk.

"They're too *quick* for me!
But now I've got them *trapped!*"
Marsh Hawk backed right up against the chipmunk hole.
His broad back blocked the entrance.
"I'm not going to move until those chipmunks come
out!
I've got them *now!*"

Marsh Hawk called over his shoulder.
"Hey you guys.
You still got those fat fat little tummies?"

The chipmunks were very quiet.
"Yeah.
I'm going to eat those fat fat little tummies, for sure."

The chipmunks crept up to the hole's entrance.
Marsh Hawk's big feathered back was blocking the whole
thing.
The chipmunks poked at Marsh Hawk's back.
They poked ...
they poked ...
one of them pulled.
"Hey you guys.
Look.
Marsh Hawk's feathers come out."
"What?"
The chipmunks clustered around.
They began to pull.
They pulled ...
"They *do!*
They come right out!"
Those chipmunks began to sing a mocking song and pull.
"Uwi ha hi
Uwi ha hi
We can pull feathers out of Marsh Hawk's back!"

They sang and pulled
and sang and pulled.

Marsh Hawk began to feel chilly back there.
>"My *back* feels cold.
>What's ..."

Marsh Hawk felt his back.
>"OH!"
>My *feathers* are gone!
>OH!
>My back is *naked!*"

Marsh Hawk flew off in a hurry.
He flew here.
He flew there.
His back was so cold.
Marsh Hawk found an old rabbit skin.
"This will help."
He pulled fur out of that rabbit skin and pasted it on his back.
Some on this side.
Some on that side.
>"Ohhh.
>That's better."

Now he wasn't cold anymore.

Marsh Hawk flew back to the chipmunk village.
>"Hey you guys.
>With your fat fat little tummies.
>I bet your tummies are tough!
>I bet your tummies taste just terrible!
>Who'd want to eat your skinny old tummies anyway."

Marsh Hawk flew away.
He never did come back.

But if you see Marsh Hawk today,
take a good look at his back.
You'll see the big patch of rabbit fur he stuck on
Where the chipmunks pulled off all his feathers that day.

Tips for Telling

This story includes a bit of slang in Marsh Hawk's comments. This is faithful to the Athabaskan source. The Athabaskan teller probably saw Marsh Hawk as resembling some bossy man he had known. The chipmunks, of course, are cute little fellows—fast, sassy, and self-confident.

I repeat Marsh Hawk's song several times as he tries to entice the chipmunks out of their hole. I have simplified Marsh Hawk's song. Here is the original, which you may prefer.

Uwi ha hi uwi ha hi hunu-dili-ggasha.	Uwi ha hi uwi ha hi I wish you'd come out.
Uwi ha hi uwi ha hi hunu-dili-jexa.	Uwi ha hi uwi ha hi Come out and stand up barking.
Uwi ha hi uwi ha hi hunu-dili-ggasha!	Uwi ha hi uwi ha hi I wish you'd come out.

About the Story

This was inspired by an Athabaskan story told by Alexie Evan in *Dena'ina Sukdu'a: Traditional Stories of the Tanaina Athabaskans,* recorded and transcribed by Joan M. Tenenbaum and Mary J. McGary (Fairbanks: Alaska Native Language Center, University of Alaska, 1984).

The tale includes Motif K606.2 *Escape by persuading captors to dance.* MacDonald's *Storyteller's Sourcebook* lists several variants of this story: Eskimo, Byelorussian, Cherokee, and Makah. Stith Thompson's *Motif-Index of Folk-Literature* shows this motif occurring in South Africa, the Cape Verde Islands, and Indonesia.

Gecko

Once a drought came to the forest.
All the animals were so thirsty.
There was no water to drink at all.
The people were thirsty too.

At last one woman said.
"We must find water in some way.
Here is the dry stream bed where the river once ran.
Surely if the strongest animals dig, we can find water.
My beautiful daughter here will marry the one who brings us
    water and saves us from this thirst."

The animals gathered to consider the offer.
That girl was so beautiful.
And perhaps the woman was right.
Perhaps they *could* dig for water in the dry stream bed.

To make the contest fair, the animals felt that everyone
    should dig in the same way.
Warthog said:
        "Dig with our tusks!
        Dig with our tusks!"
"That's the way!" agreed Elephant.
But Rhino said:
        "No! Dig with our horns!
        That's the way."
"I don't agree!" shouted Hippo.
"We should *stomp* in the dirt!"
"That's not fair," said Python.
"I don't have any legs!"

At last the animals took a vote.
It was decided that they would dig for water by stomping
    with their hind legs.

This seemed fair to everyone but Python.
Python was unhappy, but he was outvoted.

Elephant stepped into the dry stream bed.
"I am the largest.
So I will try first."
He began to stomp.
        "Elephant! Elephant!
        Heavy Heavy Heavy!
        Elephant! Elephant!
        Water Water Water."
Elephant stomped and stomped.
He chanted and chanted.
No water appeared.
After a while Elephant got tired.
        "I give up.
        There's no water here."
Elephant quit.

Other large animals wanted to try.
Hippo took a turn.
        "Hippo! Hippo!
        Heavy Heavy Heavy
        Hippo! Hippo!
        Water Water Water!"
Hippo stomped and stomped.
No water came.
At last Hippo wore out.
        "I give up.
        There's no water here."
Hippo quit.

All of the big animals had a turn.
No one could find water.

The middle-sized animals began to try.
Monkey had a turn.
And Rabbit.

Iguana had a turn too.
No one could bring water.

At last even the small animals tried.
Rat tried.
Guinea Pig tried.

When Monkey saw those small animals starting to stomp, he
    said:
        "We might as well all go home.
        If the big animals couldn't do it,
        those small ones don't have a chance."

Eventually every animal had tried.
All had failed to bring water.
The animals started to leave.
But one tiny animal spoke up.
        "I didn't have a turn.
        I didn't get a turn yet.
        Let *me* have a turn."
It was *Gecko* ... the tiny little lizard.
Gecko's friend Big Lizard started to laugh at that.
        "A puny little thing like *you*?
        Don't be ridiculous!
        You'll just make a fool of yourself."
But Gecko wanted to try.
        "I don't think we should give up yet.
        I don't want to quit.
        Let *me* try."

The animals had stomped a deep hole into the bottom of the
    dry stream bed.
Gecko climbed down into the hole.
He was so tiny you could barely see him down in that hole.
But he began to stomp.
        "Gecko Gecko
        Heavy Heavy Heavy
        Gecko Gecko

Water Water Water!''

The other animals came back to watch this tiny little gecko
    dancing around in that big hole.
They laughed and pointed.
    "Look at that silly little Gecko.
    His back is all bent over.
    He is so scrawny."
They laughed and laughed.
Gecko felt embarrassed.
But he didn't stop dancing.
    "I can't help the way I look.
    Everybody's laughing at me.
    I can't help the way I look.
    Everybody's laughing at me."
Poor little Gecko.
He felt so bad.
But he kept right on stomping in that hole.
    "Gecko! Gecko!
    Heavy Heavy Heavy
    Gecko! Gecko!
    Water Water Water!''

Gecko danced and danced.
He wouldn't stop.
After a long while someone called out
    "Look! There's some mud down by Gecko's feet.
    It looks wet there."
At that Big Lizard fell right over laughing.
    "I know what happened," said Big Lizard.
    "Gecko probably peed in his pants!''
Poor Gecko.
Now everyone was laughing harder than ever.

But Gecko did not stop.
His face was so red.
But he kept right on dancing.
    "Gecko! Gecko!

Heavy Heavy Heavy!
Gecko! Gecko!
Water Water Water!"

And do you know it really *was* water coming into the hole.
He hadn't peed in his pants at all.
It really *was* water!
It came right in...
up to his little knees.
Gecko was splashing and singing.
"Gecko! Gecko! Gecko!
Heavy heavy heavy!
Gecko! Gecko! Gecko!
Water water water!"

All the animals came running back to see what was
    happening.
"It's Gecko.
He's found water!"

Elephant came trumpeting right down into the stream bed.
He grabbed little Gecko in his trunk
and *threw* him into the bushes.
Then Elephant began to stomp in the hole.
"Elephant! Elephant!
Heavy Heavy Heavy!
Elephant! Elephant!
Water Water Water!"

But the woman stood up.
"That elephant is not the one who found the water.
Get him out of there.
Bring back Gecko!"
So Elephant left in disgrace.
Gecko was brought back from the bushes where Elephant
    had tossed him.
His little leg had been hurt when he was thrown.
"Do you think you can still dance?"

"I can try."

Little Gecko slowly climbed back down into the hole.
He began to dance once more.
>   "Gecko! Gecko!
>   Heavy Heavy Heavy
>   Gecko! Gecko!
>   Water Water Water!"

And this time everyone chanted *with* him.
>   "GECKO! GECKO!
>   HEAVY HEAVY HEAVY!
>   GECKO! GECKO!
>   WATER WATER WATER!"

Here came the water!
Up to his waist!
Up to his chin!
Gecko had to scramble out of that hole.
It filled with cool clear water!
There was water for everyone,
even for Elephant.
And tiny Gecko...
Gecko who would not give up...
He was the one who married the beautiful girl.

Tips for Telling

Let your audience tell you which animals tried to dance for water. Vary the pacing and pitch of your chant to match the animal's demeanor. The audience may want to chant with you. At any rate, encourage them to join you in the chanting when Gecko's turn comes. Avoid letting any other very tiny animals dance, so that Gecko's small size will be a contrast to his larger competitors. When the animals make fun of him, he prances nervously:

>   I can't help the way I look.
>   Everybody's laughing at me.

He returns to his deliberate stomp for water:

> GE-ko! GE-ko!
> HEA-vy...HEA-vy...HEA-vy!

If offering a girl as a prize annoys you, change the prize. Or tell the story as it is and ask for discussion of the matter after the telling. Omit Big Lizard's comment about peeing in the pants if that isn't appropriate for your audience. Both these elements were in my tale source, and I kept them.

About the Story

This story was inspired by "Chameleon and Elephant" found in *Hare and Hornbill* by Okot p'Bitek (London: Heinemann Books, 1978), pp. 5-9. P'Bitek's tales are drawn from Lango and Acoli sources. In this story the chant given is:

> Heavy one, heavy one,
> Let me see if there is any water here,
> Heavy one, strong one
> Let me see if there is any water here.

The tale includes an extended ending in which Elephant arrives and crushes Chameleon with his foot, but the wife is already pregnant with Chameleon's child. When the child is grown, his mother tells him the story of his true father, whom he avenges by setting fire to the grass and burning all the elephants. Chameleon and his mother look for the elephant that killed Chameleon, and when he is discovered they find that Chameleon is still alive between his toes. "... And they all went home rejoicing," the story ends.

I use the term *gecko* in my story rather than chameleon because I like the word's sound and because the Hawaiian clothing brand Gecko has made that small lizard popular with today's children.

Stories of digging for water in times of drought appear in many cultures. See Motif A2233.1 *Animals refuse to dig well* in MacDonald's *Storyteller's Sourcebook* for stories from

Cherokee, African-American, and African traditions. For an Australian Aborigine tale of digging for water, see "Why Koala Has No Tail" in *Look Back and See: Twenty Lively Tales for Gentle Tellers* by Margaret Read MacDonald (New York: The H.W. Wilson Co., 1991).

Kudu Break!

There was a chief who had three wives.
One day that chief caught a turtle.
>"Aaah! Delicious! I will have turtle stew!"

The chief took the turtle to Wife Number One.
>"Here, Wife. Make some turtle stew for my supper."

But Wife Number One wouldn't touch that turtle.
>"Phew ... a disgusting turtle.
>A stinky old turtle.
>I don't touch a disgusting turtle.
>Take that thing to Wife Number Two."

So the chief took his turtle to Wife Number Two.
>"Here, Wife. Make some turtle stew for my supper."

Wife Number Two also refused to touch the turtle.
>"Phew ... a disgusting turtle.
>A stinky old turtle.
>I don't touch a disgusting turtle either.
>Take that thing to Wife Number Three."

So the chief went to Wife Number Three.
Wife Number Three was the little one.
She was the youngest wife.
It was she who did most of the work around there.
>"Here Wife. Clean this turtle and cook it for my
>   evening meal."

>"Yes, Husband.
>I will cook this turtle for you."

Wife Number Three took the turtle.
She cleaned it.
She took off the shell.
She put the bones into a pot and cooked them.
She cooked it a long time, until it was very tender.
She had made a very tasty turtle stew.

Then she put the stew in a little clay bowl along with its
    gravy.
She covered the bowl with a little grass mat so the insects
    could not get into it.
She set it on a high wall so the dogs and cats could not reach
    it.
Then she went to the veld to do her work gathering broom
    grass.

While Wife Number Three was away working,
Wife Number One passed by her house.
She smelled that turtle stew.
    "I wonder if Wife Number Three is a good cook?"
Wife Number One went into the house.
She took down the bowl of stew.
She took off the covering mat.
She dipped her finger into the gravy.
    "Mmm ... mmm ... Delicious!"
Wife Number One ate a piece of the turtle.
    "Turtle alive is disgusting.
    But turtle cooked is *delicious!*"
She ate another piece.
Soon that woman had eaten up all the stew.
Wife Number One put the covering back on the bowl, set it
    back on the high wall, and went on her way.

That evening, Wife Number Three returned from the veld.
She took her little bowl of stew and went to her husband.
"Here, Big Man," she said. "Here is your turtle stew."
And she gave him the little clay dish with the mat covering.
Her husband smiled and smacked his lips.
    "Mmmmmm!"
But when he lifted the covering ...
    "Yo!" Only an empty dish!
    "Wife! You have eaten my stew!"

    "It was not I.
    I was working in the veld.

And look, I covered the stew with a mat so not even
    the dogs and cats could get into it."

"I do not believe you.
This stew is gone!"

"But I speak the truth.
It was not I who ate that stew."

The husband was so angry.
His stomach was black with hunger.
    "I will go to the Wise Man of the village.
    He will consult his magic bones.
    They will tell whether or not you speak the truth."

So he went to the Wise Man.
And when the case had been heard,
the Wise Man cast his handful of magic bones on the ground
    and read them.

"There is a test which will tell whether your wife speaks the
    truth.
Go home and weave a strong rope from the sinews of a kudu
    antelope.
Choose two strong men and send one to each side of the
    river, where the water rushes past.
Let one hold each end of that kudu rope.
Then this Wife Number Three must walk across that rope.
If the rope breaks and she falls into the water,
we will know that she was guilty.
But if she passes across the river without falling,
that one is innocent."

The husband did as the Wise Man suggested.
And when the kudu rope was ready, all of the villagers came
    to the river to watch this test.
Beneath the rope, the river swished dangerously ...
    Shoo ... shoo. Shoo ... shoo.

Wife Number Three began to walk ... so carefully.
And as she walked she chanted.

> "Kudu break.
> Kudu break.
> If I ate it ...
> Kudu break.
>
> Kudu break.
> Kudu break.
> Husband's turtle ...
> Kudu break."

Walking and chanting, chanting and walking ...
she passed to the other side.
The rope of kudu sinews did not break.

> "Aaaaah. This one is innocent.
> We are sorry we accused you, Wife Number Three.
> You may sit down.
> Was there another wife in the house?
> Wife Number Two.
> Come and cross the rope.
> Perhaps you are the guilty person."

Those strong men held the rope taut.
Beneath, the waters swished past so dangerously.
> *Shoo ... shoo. Shoo ... shoo.*
Wife Number Two began to cross the rope.

> "Kudu break.
> Kudu break.
> If I ate it ...
> Kudu break.
>
> Kudu break.
> Kudu break.
> Husband's turtle ...

Kudu break."

Walking and chanting, chanting and walking,
she crossed that river.
And the rope of kudu sinews did not break.

"Aaaah! Wife Number Two!
You are innocent.
We are sorry we accused you.
You may sit down.
Who else was in the house?
Wife Number One!
Perhaps it was you."

The strong men held the rope taut.
Beneath the river swished dangerously.
Shoo ... shoo. Shoo ... shoo.
Wife Number One began to cross the rope.
Wife Number One remembered that turtle stew.
She remembered how delicious it had tasted.
She chanted ...

"Kudu don't break.
Kudu don't break.
If I ate it ...
Kudu don't break.

Husband's turtle.
Disgusting turtle.
Delicious turtle ..."

"Delicious turtle?" cried the people.
"What is that woman saying?"

But the rope of kudu sinew had had enough.
With a snap it *broke.*
And the guilty woman fell into the river.

Then the little turtles of the river all began to swim around
    that Wife Number One,
nibbling on that wife and saying
        "Disgusting Wife!
        Disgusting Wife!
        Disgusting Wife!
        Delicious Wife!"

Now in that village there is a saying.
        "If a thing is yours,
        you may stoop to it.
        If a thing is not yours,
        stand straight and pass it by."
This stew was not hers,
yet the woman stooped to it.
And so, of course, she was punished.

Tips for Telling

This tale lends itself to enactment. When the wives cross the river, I ask the audience to swish their hands together saying *"Shoo ... shoo. Shoo ... shoo"* to simulate the swishing river.

An audience member holds each end of the imaginary rope. And I select "wives" from the audience to attempt the crossing while the audience "swishes" beneath them. I hold the crossing "wife" by the shoulders behind and guide her across, saying her chant for her. I then address her on behalf of the audience. "We are sorry we accused you. You may sit down."

If you are including this story in a program, you will want to use it toward the end. Once children have engaged in this sort of "acting out," they want to act out *every* story.

About the Story

A wonderful variant of this story appears in *Tales from the Basotho* by Minnie Postma (Austin: Published for the American Folklore Society by the University of Texas, 1974), pp. 53-57. The motif of crossing a rope as a test of innocence is found in several African tales. Stith Thompson's *Motif-Index of Folk-Literature* lists under Motif H225 *Ordeal by rope-walking* Basuto, Ekoi, and Jamaican variants. Kenneth Clarke's *A Motif-Index of the Folktales of Culture-Area V West Africa* (Ann Arbor: University Microfilms International, 1958) gives two Ikom sources and one Ekoi source.

What Are Their Names!

A girl got married.
Her husband had four brothers.
Four brothers-in-law.
That girl did not know their names.

The first day she took her cassava.
She pounded it.
She put it on the fire and cooked it.
She made fungi.*
The girl took that mush to her brothers-in-law.
She set it in front of them.

They said "Your mush looks good.
But you did not say our names.
Say our names.
Then we will eat your mush."

That girl was so embarrassed.
She did not know the names of her husband's brothers.
She took her mush.
She went back home.

Next day when the girl was pounding her mush,
a little bird lit in the tree above her.
The bird began to sing.
>"Look at that girl
>(she *pounds* she *pounds*)
>She doesn't know their names.
>(she *pounds* she *pounds*)
>Four brothers-in-law.
>(she *pounds* she *pounds*)
>She doesn't know their names!"

"Get out of here, you screeching bird!"

* *A porridge made of cassava flour*

The girl waved her pestle at it.
But the bird kept on singing.
>"Listen, I will tell you!
>(she *pounds* she *pounds*)
>One is Tumba Sikundu!
>(she *pounds* she *pounds*)
>One is Tumba Sikundu Muna!

>Listen, I will tell you!
>(she *pounds* she *pounds*)
>One is Tumba Kaulu!
>(she *pounds* she *pounds*)
>One is Tumba Kaulu Muna!"

"Get *out* of here, bird!
Stop that racket!"
The girl threw her pestle at him and drove him off.

That night she cooked the mush.
She took it to her brothers-in-law.
She set it in front of them.

"Your mush looks good.
Say our names,
then we will eat your mush."

That girl was still embarrassed.
She did not *know* their names.
She took her mush and went home.

The next day she was pounding her fungi again.
Here came that little bird.
>"Listen, I will tell you
>(she *pounds* she *pounds*)
>One is Tumba Sikundu!
>(she *pounds* she *pounds*)
>One is Tumba Sikundu Muna!

Listen, I will tell you
(she *pounds* she *pounds*)
One is Tumba Kaulu!
(she *pounds* she *pounds*)
One is Tumba Kaulu Muna!''

"Stop that *racket!*" screamed the girl.
And she threw her pestle at the bird again.

Then she went on pounding.
"One is Tumba....
Oh, *my!*
What was that little bird singing?
Was he singing the *names?*

If only I can remember....
What was he saying....
One is Tumba ... Sikundu?
Yes!
One is Tumba ... Sikundu ... Muna!
That's *it!*
Two more....
One is Tumba ... *Kaulu!*
One is Tumba Kaulu ... *Muna!*
Those are their *names!*"

The girl ran home.
She cooked her mush.
She took it to the home of her brothers-in-law.
She set it in front of them.

"Your mush looks good.
But say our names.
Then we will eat your mush."

The girl smiled. "You must be ... Tumba Sikundu!
And *you* are Tumba Sikundu Muna!
You would be ... Tumba Kaulu.

And *you* are Tumba Kaulu Muna!''

''That's *right!*
You have learned our names.
Now we will eat your mush.
Thank you, sister-in-law.''

This is the story of a girl
Who did not know the names of her brothers-in-law.
But when she went to pound her fungi
A little bird told her.

I have told my little tale.
It is finished.

Tips for Telling

When telling this tale try to get your audience pounding out the rhythm as the girl pounds her mush. We are all pounding together as the bird speaks, *"Look* at that *girl"* (she *pounds* she *pounds*) ... we bring our fist down even harder as the bird says "pounds." Keep the pounding going throughout the bird's calls.

Here is a sample chant. Pound on every capitalized syllable:

> LISten, I will TELL you
> (she POUNDS she POUNDS)
> ONE is Tumba SIkundu!
> (she POUNDS she POUNDS)
> ONE is Tumba SIkundu MuNA!

You might use this story to start a unit about names. Read or tell other stories of the magic of names. See MacDonald's *Storyteller's Sourcebook* subject index under "Names" for many such tales. Continue by studying the meaning of names and the history of family names. Collect the stories that go with nicknames and pet names used by people your students know.

About the Story

This telling is elaborated from "A Bride and Her Brothers-in-Law" collected by Heli Chatelain in *Folk-Tales of Angola: Fifty Tales with Ki-Mbundu Text, Literal English Translation, Introduction, and Notes* (Boston and New York: Published for the American Folk-Lore Society by G.E. Stechert & Co., 1894), pp. 141-145. Chatelain had been a United States Commercial Agent in Loanda, West Africa.

World folklore contains many stories of the magic in guessing names, best known perhaps is "Rumplestiltskin" (Motif D2183). MacDonald's *Storyteller's Sourcebook* mentions also several Caribbean tales in which Old Woman Crim is defeated by guessing her name (C432.1.2), a Native American tale in which Skunny Wunny defeats fox by guessing his name (C432.1.3), and a Yoruba tale in which the King of the Spirit World is defeated when Tintinyin learns his identity from an ega bird (B216.4).

Since our story involves a newlywed, it may be more closely related to Motif H323 *Suiter Test: Learning Girl's Name*. MacDonald's *Storyteller's Sourcebook* includes variants from Nigeria, Ghana, and Jamaica of a story in which Tortoise, Lizard, or Ananse listen and overhear three girls calling each other by name. In a Luban variant, Swallow tells Muskrat the secret name of a tree, allowing Muskrat to wed the chief's daughter.

Aayoga with Many Excuses

Aayoga was the most beautiful girl in her village.
She *knew* just how beautiful she was.
Every day Aayoga would sit and gaze at her reflection.
Her mirror was a shiny brass bowl.
In its bottom she could see her pretty face reflected.
>"Just *look* at my dainty little eyebrows!
>Just *look* at my red little mouth!
>Just *look* at my rosy rosy cheeks!
>It's no wonder everyone says I am beautiful!"

One day her mother called to her
>"Aayoga, go down to the stream and bring some
>   water please.
>I want to make some cherrycakes."

But Aayoga could not be bothered.
And that girl had an excuse for everything.
>"Oh Mother, I couldn't do that...
>I might fall in the stream and drown."

>"Just hang onto a branch, Aayoga.
>You will be all right."

>"Oh no, I couldn't do that ...
>The branch might break."

>"Then hang onto a stout branch."

>"Oh no, I couldn't do that ...
>My mittens might tear."

>"Then you could mend your mittens."

>"Oh no, I couldn't do that ...
>My mittens are made of leather.

The needle might break."

"Then use a bigger needle."

"Oh no, I couldn't do that ...
I might prick my finger."

"Then put on a leather thimble."

"Oh no, I couldn't do that ...
It would pinch my little finger."

Her mother was too frustrated.
"Then never mind, Aayoga.
I'll send your *sister*."
And she did.

Aayoga's sister brought water from the stream.
Her mother made lovely cherrycakes.
When they had finished baking they smelled so good.
At last Aayoga looked up from her mirror.
"Give me a cherrycake, Mother.
They smell delicious."

"Oh Aayoga," said her mother, "I couldn't do that ...
They are still hot.
You might burn your little hands."

"That's no problem, mother.
I will wear my mittens."

"Oh no, you couldn't do that ...
You might get your mittens dirty."

"That's no problem,
I could wash them."

"Oh no, you couldn't do that ...

They would get all wet."

"That's no problem,
I could put them in the sun to dry."

"Oh no, you couldn't do that ...
The sun would make the leather stiff."

"That's no problem.
I could beat them with a stick to soften them again."

"Oh no, you couldn't do that ...
You might get a splinter in your pretty little hands."

"No Aayoga, you must not touch these cherrycakes.
They are too dangerous for a delicate beauty like yourself.
I will give them to your sister."

And her mother gave Aayoga's sister a large cherrycake.
The girl took the cherrycake down to the stream and sat on
    the stream bank to munch her cake.
Aaoyga came and sat near her.
Aayoga began to stretch her little neck out
        looking ... looking...
        looking ... at her sister's cherrycake.
Her little neck seemed to grow longer and longer each time
    she cast a jealous look at that cherrycake.
        "It's OK, Aayoga," said her sister.
        "Here, you can have the rest."
And she reached out the half-eaten cherrycake.
Aayoga was *furious!*
        "You think I want that cake
        after you have been slobbering over it?
        Get out of here with your old cherrycake!"
And Aayoga began to flap her arms at her sister.
        "Go ... go ... go ... go ... *go!*
        Go ... go ... go ... go ... *go!"*
The sister jumped up and ran.

But Aayoga followed her making shooing motions.

"Go ... go ... go ... go ... *go!*
Go ... go ... go ... go ... *go!*"

Aayoga became more and more excited.

She flapped her arms more and more rapidly.

"Go ... go ... go ... go ...
Go ... go ... go ... go ...
Go ... go ... go ... go ... *go!*"

Then something began to happen to that girl.

She was flapping her arms like bird's wings.

Suddenly feathers started to form on her arms.

She kept stretching her long neck out to see that cherrycake.

Her neck began to lengthen into a goose's neck.

Aayoga was turning into a *goose!*

"Go ... go ... go ... go ...
Go ... go ... go ... go ...
Go ... go ... go ... go ... *go!*"

That silly girl fell over right into the stream!

But not a bit did it matter!

For her arms were now wings,

her body was now the body of a great white goose!

And what a beautiful bird it was.

The goose began at once to admire itself in the water.

"Just *look* what a beautiful yellow beak I have!
Just *look* what smooth white feathers I have!
Just *look what* lovely darting eyes I have!"

To this day the white goose swims on the banks of that
    stream.

She turns her long neck this way and that, admiring her
    beautiful reflection in the stream.

And so that no one will ever forget her name, she calls
    constantly

"Ayooooga-ga-ga-ga-gaaaa!
Ayooooga-ga-ga-ga-gaaa!
Ayooooga-ga-ga-ga-gaaa!"

That is the story of Aayoga who made excuses.

Tips for Telling

When telling this story I carry on the conversation between mother and daughter by turning my body just slightly to the right and then to the left as I look at the imaginary mother and then at the daughter. This eliminates the necessity of stating "said the daughter" and "said the mother" after each line. I do not change my voice for the two characters, but I do change my tone. The mother is strict and put out with her lazy daughter. The girl is whining and trying to think up excuses. When Aayoga changes into a goose I flap my arms a bit and stretch out my neck while making the goose's call.

"Aayoga" could make an interesting playlet for a small group of students to perform.

About the Story

This tale is inspired by a Nanai folktale in *Folktales of the Amur: Stories from the Russian Far East* by Dmitri Nagishkin (illustrated by Gennady Pavlishin and translated by Emily Lehrman, New York: Harry N. Abrams, Inc., 1980). If possible, obtain this book so you can show Pavlishin's lovely illustration of Aayoga in her transformation. I have elaborated the story considerably but left out the fact that Aayoga is the daughter of "A Nanai of the Samarov clan named La."

The Nanai story presents interesting development with its banter between daughter and mother, and the daughter's gradual change into goose form. See also "Aloga" in *The Sun Maiden and the Crescent Moon: Siberian Folktales* by James Riordan (New York: Interlink Books, 1989).

This unusual story has an interesting parallel in Tinguian tales from the Philippines. In one a child, impatient because food takes too long to cook, makes nipa leaf wings and turns into a dove (MacDonald, *Storyteller's Sourcebook* Motif A1948.1). In others a lazy bride or a lazy boy become birds (Motif A1999.4.1). Many European tales are told of a baker's daughter who objects to the large size of the dough to be given to a beggar (Jesus) and is turned into an owl or woodpecker (Motif A1958.0.1).

Kanu Above
and Kanu Below

Kanu Below was a chief.
He lived on this earth.
Kanu Above was a God.
He lived in the skies.

Now Kanu Below had a beautiful daughter.
He cared for her more than for all his wealth.
How he loved that child.
But one day Kanu Above reached down and took the child
    away.
He carried her off to the sky and kept her there.

Kanu Below wept and wept.
He could not be comforted.
In his sorrow he forgot to look over his people.
His under-chiefs began to take more and more responsibility
    for the village.
One day those chiefs came to him and said
        "Kanu! Kanu Below!
        A stranger has come into our village.
        His name is Spider.
        That person is causing much trouble.
        He weaves sticky webs over everyone's doorways.
        He leaves webs across the paths.
        People are tripping and falling.
        People keep stumbling into spider webs.
        You must send this person from the village.
        We do not want him here."

Kanu looked up from his grief.
        "I will handle this problem.
        Tell Spider to come here."

To Spider he said

> "Spider, you must not leave webs across the paths.
>
> People will trip and hurt themselves.
>
> You must not spin webs across the doorways.
>
> People will stumble into them.
>
> Do you understand?"

To the chiefs he said

> "See this Spider?
>
> This Spider does some things we do not like.
>
> But this Spider has much good in him.
>
> We will keep him in the village.
>
> We will keep him among us."

And it was so.

Two days later the chiefs came again to Kanu.

> "Kanu! Kanu Below!
>
> A stranger has come into the village.
>
> His name is Rat.
>
> This Rat is sneaking into people's houses.
>
> He is taking rice.
>
> He is taking meat.
>
> He is taking kola nuts.
>
> This Rat cannot stay in our village.
>
> Tell him to go."

Kanu said, "Tell Rat to come here."

To Rat he said

> "Rat, you must not go into people's houses and take
> things that are not yours.
>
> They are hungry too.
>
> Do not take their rice.
>
> Do not take their meat.
>
> Do not take their kola nuts.
>
> Do you understand?"

To the chiefs he said

> "See this Rat?
>
> He does some things we do not like.
>
> But there is much good in Rat.

We will keep him in the village.
We will keep Rat among us."
And it was so.

Two days later the chiefs came again.
"Kanu! Kanu Below!
A stranger is in this village.
His name is Anteater.
He is causing trouble.
This Anteater is digging holes in everyone's yard.
People are falling into them and breaking their legs.
Send this Anteater out of the village.
He cannot stay here."

Kanu said, "Tell Anteater to come here."
To Anteater he said
"Anteater,
you must stop digging holes in people's yards.
People are falling.
They are hurting their legs.
You must stop doing this.
Do you understand?"
To the chiefs he said
"See this Anteater?
He does some things we do not like.
But there is much good in this Anteater.
We should keep him in the village.
We must keep him among us."
And it was so.

Two days later the chiefs came again
"Kanu! Kanu Below!
There is a stranger in the village.
His name is Fly.
He is driving everyone crazy.
He buzzes around our heads.
He bites us on the neck.
He bites us on the behind.

Send him away from here.
Get him out of our village."

Kanu said, "Tell Fly to come here."
To Fly he said
    "Fly, you must not buzz around people's heads.
    This is very annoying to people.
    You must not bite them on the neck.
    You must not bite them on the behind.
    This hurts our people.
    Do you understand?"
To the chiefs he said
    "See this Fly?
    He does some things we do not like, yes.
    But there is much good in this Fly.
    We must keep him in the village.
    We should keep him among us."
And it was so.

Days passed, and Kanu was still so sad for the loss of his
    daughter.

One day he said
    "If only someone from our village could climb to the
      sky and speak to Kanu Above.
    Perhaps he could be persuaded to return my
      daughter."
Kanu Above was powerful.
Kanu Above was frightening.
None of the chiefs was willing to approach him.
They kept silent.
But Spider spoke up.
    "Kanu Below, I could go for you.
    I could spin a web and climb to the sky.
    I like the way you treated me.
    I will help you."

Rat said
> "Me too.
> I will go.
> I like the way you treated me, Kanu.
> I want to help."

Anteater said
> "Don't forget me.
> Let me help also.
> I like the way you treated me, Kanu.
> I am going to help."

Fly said
> "And I will go along too.
> I like the way you treated me, Kanu.
> Now I am going to help."

Spider spun a web right up to the sky.
He fastened it to a cloud.
The four friends climbed up and began to walk around in the
    sky country
looking for Kanu Above.
There was his court!
> "Kanu! Kanu Above!
> We have come from Kanu Below.
> He misses his daughter so much.
> We ask that you return her."

Kanu Above glared at these intruders.
He was angry.
But he said:
> "Well, sit down.
> We shall see."
Kanu Above called the women
> "Go and prepare food for our guests."
But to one woman he whispered something in private.
Fly said, "This might be a job for me."
Fly followed that woman.

He watched.
The women prepared rice.
They prepared palm oil sauce.
They prepared meat sauce.
That woman took poison.
She poured it into the meat sauce.

Fly hurried back to his three friends.
He buzzed in their ears.
"Don't touch the meat.
It is poisoned."
"Don't touch the meat.
They poisoned it."
"The meat is poisoned.
Don't touch it."

The food was placed before them.
There was a bowl of rice.
There was a bowl of palm oil sauce.
There was a bowl of meat sauce.

"Thank you for the food," said the friends.
"But in our country we never eat meat."
They pushed away the meat sauce and ate only the palm oil.

Kanu Above looked at them.
"Are these people clever? Or what?"
Kanu Above said
"Now you may rest in this house."
They went into a house.
Kanu's servants closed the doors.
Kanu's servants closed the windows.
They were locked inside that house.
They waited one ... two ... three ... four... five ... six days.
No one brought them food.
No one brought them water.

Rat said, "This is a job for me."

Rat gnawed a hole.
He went out.
Rat went into one house.
He took rice.
He brought it back.
He went into another house.
He took meat.
He brought it back.
Rat went into Kanu's house.
He took kola nuts.
He brought them back.
The friends ate and were healthy again.

Kanu's men saw that they were still alive.
They brought brush to set fire to the house.

Anteater said, "Here is a job for me!"
Anteater began to dig.
Fast, fast, he dug.
He dug a hole right under the wall.
The four friends escaped.

They went before Kanu Above.
They brought with them one kola nut.
        "Here is a kola nut.
        We give it to you.
        Our house burned down.
        May we take back the child now?"

Kanu Above wondered
        "Are these people clever? Or what?"
"I will bring the child," he said.
"But you must choose her.
If she is really yours you will know her."

He sent the women to dress the girls.
There were twenty young girls.
They would all be dressed alike.

The friends were worried.
They had never seen Kanu Below's daughter.
How would they know her?

Fly said, "This is a job for me again."
He followed the women.
He watched them dress the girls.
They put beads around their necks.
They put bracelets on their wrists.
They put anklets on their feet.
They braided their hair just so.

But one girl, they ignored.
No one helped her.
She had to put on her own beads.
She had to put on her own bracelets.
She had to put on her own anklets.
She had to fix her hair all by herself.

Fly said, "That must be our chief's daughter.
She is not from this place.
They treat her poorly."

Fly flew back to his friends.
He buzzed in their ears.
  "The girl who jumps.
  She is the one."

  "Grab the girl who jumps."
  "Watch for the girl who jumps.
  That will be the one."

They brought out twenty young girls.
They were all dressed just alike.
They were lovely in their beads and bracelets.
Fly buzzed around their heads.
  "Not this one ... not this one ... not this one...."
Suddenly he *bit* one girl.

"Whoop!" she jumped.
The friends grabbed her.
 "This is the one.
 We choose *this* one."

Kanu Above stared and stared.
 "Are these people clever? Or what?
 Well then, you may have that girl.
 Take her to your chief.
 And here are four kola nuts
 to show my admiration for his four friends."

They took the girl and climbed down to their country again.

Kanu Below was so happy ... so happy ... to have his
 daughter home again.

He called all the people in the village.
 "See what these four have done," he said.
 "This is Spider.
 You wanted to send him away.
 This is Rat.
 You did not want him in the village.
 This is Anteater.
 You did not want him around.
 This is Fly.
 You would have banished him forever.
 Yet these are the ones who have brought back my
  daughter.
 To me these four are without price.
 It is these four who will be my chiefs in the future."

And it was so.

This is the story of Kanu Above and Kanu Below.

Tips for Telling

When telling this story I like to address a child in the audience as "Spider," another as "Fly," etc. I chide "Spider" for making those webs all over the place and ask him not to do it again.

Then turning to the audience as a whole, I admonish them to keep this Spider among us. Later I point out Spider, Fly, and the others as our new chiefs. When Fly buzzes and bites the girl, I pinch one of the girls and whisper to her "jump."

This is a fine story which has much to say to us about working with our troublemakers rather than banishing them from our group. I prepared the tale especially for a mentoring group which was recently founded on the island where we summer. Some young boys had broken into homes, stealing money and guns. The island's response was to start a mentor program to "keep their youth among them."

About the Story

This tale uses elements of "The girl taken by Kanu" and "Kanu above and Kanu below" in *Limba Stories and Story-telling* by Ruth Finnegan (New York: Oxford University Press, 1967), pp. 274-280. "Kanu above and Kanu below" was collected from Kabi Kanu September 2, 1961. "The girl taken by Kanu" was collected from Niaka Dema November 10, 1961.

There are some interesting elements which I did not use in my version. You can add them back in if you wish.

In "Kanu above and Kanu below," the girls have been beautified for the Bondo society initiation ceremony. When they arrive to be admired, Fly bites the daughter and she jumps.

In "The girl taken by Kanu," kola nuts are given as tokens when the messengers arrive and when they approach Kanu Above, and four kola nuts are sent to the chief below as a token from Kanu Above. In this tale the chief below is called simply "chief." Finnegan finds the use of the term *Kanu* for the person below unusual as that would normally refer to spirits of some sort. Kanu Above is of course a heavenly being.

The chief in "The girl taken by Kanu" says on hearing of the pests' actions: "It is good. I love men: for I am chief. Let them just stay with me."

This could be considered a variant of Motif H1385.1 *Quest for stolen princess*. However, its multiple skilled helpers make it more closely related to F601 *Extraordinary companions help hero in suitor tasks* (Type 513, 514 *The Helpers*). The most common variants of that type are the Russian tale "The Fool of the World and the Flying Ship" and the Grimms' "How Six Traveled Through the World." In those stories the helpers are men with unusual talents—Sharpshooter, Eater, Drinker, and such.

MacDonald's *Storyteller's Sourcebook* lists twenty-two variants from nineteen cultures under F601. A Hausa variant in which a chief's daughter is stolen by a robber chief and a young man gains five companions who rescue her, seems similar to our Limba tale.

The Limba variant, "The Girl Who Went to Kanu," ends with a discussion of which animal should wed the princess; they are awarded a cow instead, which they can divide. But this motif relates the story to H621 *Skillful companions create a woman. To whom does she belong?* and H621.1 *Skillful companions resuscitate girl. To whom does she belong?*

MacDonald's *Storyteller's Sourcebook* cites sources of this tale from Denmark, Greece, Russia, Poland, Czechoslovakia, Latvia, Ghana (Ashanti), North Africa, and Ethiopia (Somali) and cites variants from three west and central African sources (Liberia, Ashanti, Congolese) for H641.4 *Four skillful brothers resuscitate father.* Gerald McDermott's popular picture book *Ananse the Spider* (New York: Holt, Rinehart, and Winston, 1972) is an example of this tale.

Ko Kóngole

There was a princess who was very beautiful.
Her father brought suitors to wed her.
She rejected them all.
That girl wanted a husband she could be proud of.
She wouldn't even let those suitors sit down.

Here comes her father *(audience chants):*
> Ko! Kóngole!
> Ko! Kóngole!

(Father) "Mam'olilo, Mam'olilo!
> *(Ko! Kóngole!)*
> I've found a husband!"
> *(Ko! Kóngole!)*
(Girl) "What is his name?"
> *(Ko! Kóngole!)*
(Father) "His name is Mr. Porcupine!"
> *(Ko! Kóngole!)*

(stop rhythm)
(Girl) "Mr. *Porcupine?*
> He's too *prickly!*
> Take away the chair
> and send him *home."*
> *(Ko! Kóngole!*
> *Ko! Kóngole!)*

(Father) "Mam'olilo, Mam'olilo!
> *(Ko! Kóngole!)*
> I've found a husband."
> *(Ko! Kóngole!)*
(Girl) "What is his name?"
> *(Ko! Kóngole!)*
(Father) "His name is Mr. Antelope!"

(Ko! Kóngole!)
(stop rhythm)
(Girl) "Mr. Antelope?
      He's too jumpy.
      Take away the chair
      and send him *home.*"
      (Ko! Kóngole!
      Ko! Kóngole!)

(Repeat this pattern inserting any animals you like—elephant, leopard, lion—until you are ready to end the story.)

      "Mam'olilo, Mam'olilo!
      (Ko! Kóngole!)
      I've found a husband."
      (Ko! Kóngole!)
      "What is his name?"
      (Ko! Kóngole!)
      "His name is Mr. Rooster!"
      (Ko! Kóngole!)
      "Mr. Rooster?"
Rooster strutted up and down.
His head was high.
He was *proud.*
The girl *liked* the way he looked!
      "Rooster! Rooster!
      He can be my husband!
      Bring him a chair
      and let him sit down!"
      (Ko! Kóngole!
      Ko! Kóngole!
      Ko! Kóngole!
      Ko! Kóngole!)
The girl took a husband.
      (Ko! Kóngole!)
The girl married Rooster.
      (Ko! Kóngole!)

He was *proud!*
>   *(Ko! Kóngole!)*

(stop rhythm)
The people brought tables.
The people brought food.
The wedding feast was set.
Everyone ate.
It began to rain.
It rained and it rained.
Out in the yard
the worms came out,
came out of their holes
and wriggled on the ground.
Rooster saw that.
Worms just wriggling and wriggling in the rain.

Rooster jumped up!
Rooster ran out into the yard.
>   *"Tslk ... tslk ... tslk ... tslk...."*

Rooster began to gobble up those *worms!*
>   *(Ko! Kóngole!*
>   *Ko! Kóngole!)*

Oh what *shame!*
>   *(Ko! Kóngole!)*

Her husband eats *worms!*
>   *(Ko! Kóngole!)*

She turned away the others.
>   *(Ko! Kóngole!)*

Now she has a husband ...
>   *(Ko! Kóngole!)*

who just eats *worms!*

Tips for Telling

Start the audience chanting:

> Ko! Kóngole!
> Ko! Kóngole!

If the audience members are accustomed to participating in story-play, they may take up the chant and keep it running behind your lines throughout the story. Most audiences will need your lead between the narrative lines for each refrain. A soft hand clap accompanies the chant, if you like. It can be great fun to act this out, letting the audience provide a dancing chant as each suitor comes onstage and parades around.

The chanting *stops* when the girl looks at her suitor and begins to comment. She surveys him slowly, comments ''Porcupine? Not *him*. He's too *prickly!*'' She now takes up the chant, saying:

> Take away the chair
> and send him *home!*
>
> Ko! Kóngole!
> Ko! Kóngole!

The speed of the story picks up at the end, as Rooster is selected and the wedding arrangements take place. Story collectors Mabel Ross and Barbara Walker (cited below) say of their Nkundo teller:

> The procession of suitors having been completed, the narrator proceeds quickly and economically to the denouement.... The tumbling-over-itself of the concluding portion is suggested by the intermixture of verb tenses and the rapidity with which the events are summarized.
>
> The contrast between the orderliness of the courtship procedure and the mad

scramble accompanying the unsuitable marriage serves to underscore the moral the
narrator expects the listeners to draw from
the tale.

Deliver the tale's last sequence slowly and with great
shame.

Now she has a husband
who just eats *worms.*

About the Story

A fine variant of this story appears in *"On Another
Day ...": Tales Told Among the Nkundo of Zaire* by Mabel H.
Ross and Barbara K. Walker (Hamden, Connecticut: Archon
Books, 1979), pp. 210-215. They provide interesting notes for
the tale there.

In a variant from Nigeria, it is the king who marries a
cock's daughter and is embarrassed by her pecking (Elphinstone Dayrell, "The King Who Married the Cock's Daughter"
in *Folk Stories from Southern Nigeria,* Westport, Connecticut: Greenwood Publishing Group, 1969 [reprint of 1910
edition], pp. 42-45). The tale reminds one of the Aesop fable
that corresponds with Motif J1908.2 *Cat transformed to
maiden runs after mouse.* In this story, Jupiter (or Venus) has
turned a cat to a maid so she can wed the man she loves. The
cat's true nature is revealed when a mouse is released. Stith
Thompson's *Motif-Index of Folk-Literature* cites also a Nama
source from Africa with Motif J1908.3 *Frog-woman betrays
self by croaking.*

Animal suitors are not uncommon in African narratives.
See the tale "Onalu" in Uche Okeke, *Tales of Land of Death:
Igbo Folktales* (New York: Doubleday, 1971), pp. 66-68. And
see "Gecko" in this book.

Ningun

Ningun was the most beautiful girl in the village.

And Ningun *knew* it.

Almost every young man in the village had asked Ningun to
marry him.

>"Ningun ... would you marry me?
>
>You are *so* beautiful ..."

"Marry *you?*

Just *look* at you.

Skinny legs.

Pointy nose.

Lumpy ears.

No way would *I* marry *you.*"

And Ningun would turn away in disgust.

With every young man it was the same.

>"Oh Ningun ... you are *so* lovely.
>
>Would you marry me?"

"Would I marry *you?*

You must be joking.

You walk like a turtle.

Your hair stands up on end.

And look at your beady little eyes.

No way would *I* marry *you.*"

In this village one young hunter was stronger and more
handsome than all the rest.

Ningun's father thought surely *this* hunter would be a good
match for his proud and lovely daughter.

So the hunter came to court Ningun.

>"Ningun you are such a fine young woman.
>
>And I am the strongest hunter in the village.
>
>Would you not like to marry me?"

Ningun looked that hunter over.

She was too proud even for him.

>"You think *I* would marry *you?*

I think *not*.
Look at your big feet!
Look at your long gangly arms.
Look at your big lumpy nose!
No way would *I* marry *you.*"

The hunter was so embarrassed.
He had never thought of himself as gangly before.
He didn't know he had a lumpy nose.
And he hadn't noticed how big his feet were.
He went away in shame.

Ningun's father said
> "This has gone far enough.
> If you won't pick a husband ...
> I will pick one for you.
> If you haven't picked someone by Saturday night ...
> *I* will choose you a husband."

Now Ningun was worried.
She began to look closely at all the men in that village.
> "That one? Definitely *not.*
> This one? Oh *never.*
> The one over there? Not possible!"
And in this way she went through the entire town.

But Saturday,
at the marketplace,
Ningun saw a handsome stranger.
She had never seen this man before.
He was tall, and slim.
He moved so sinuously when he walked.
His muscles rippled under his clothing.
And he was wearing a velvet jacket of green and brown and
    gold.
It looked soooo soft.

Ningun went right up to this stranger.

"Handsome stranger.
My name is Ningun.
I'm the most beautiful girl in the village."
The stranger turned away.
But Ningun followed.
"Perhaps you don't understand.
My name is Ningun.
I'm the most beautiful girl in this village.

And I'm *available*."
The stranger looked at her.
"Who *is* this girl?"
He walked away.

Ningun still followed.
Everywhere he went that day Ningun was right behind him.
Every time he turned she was there.
"Ningun—that's me.
The most beautiful girl in the village.
Still available."

When the day was over Ningun was still right behind that
    stranger.
He started to leave the village.
Ningun followed.
At the edge of the village he turned to Ningun.
"Girl, you cannot go home with me.
Go back now.
Before it's too late."

"You are *so* handsome," said Ningun.
"I will follow you wherever you go."
The stranger turned and walked into the forest.
Ningun was right behind.
Deep into the forest she followed.

Then suddenly the stranger stopped.
He turned.

And now he was smiling at her.
But Ningun saw ...
the handsome stranger *had no teeth!*
>"Handsome stranger ...
>what has happened to your teeth?"
>"My teeth are *gone*
>and they won't come back.
>And *you* should go home
>before it's too late."

Ningun would not turn back.
>"Ohhhh ... you're even *more* handsome without your
>teeth!"

And she followed him deeper into the forest.

After a while the stranger stopped again.
Again he turned.
And Ningun saw ...
the handsome stranger had no *arms!*
>"Handsome stranger, what happened to your *arms?*"
>"My arms are *gone*
>and they won't come back.
>My teeth are gone
>and they won't come back.
>And *you* should go home
>before it's too late."

But Ningun would not give up.
>"Ohhhhh ... you're even *more* handsome without
>your arms!"

And she followed him on ... deeper into the forest.
There ... deep ... deep in the forest ... the stranger leaned up
against a huge tree.
>"Now I am home," he said.

And he turned to Ningun.
Then Ningun saw ...
the handsome stranger did not have any *legs!*
>"Handsome stranger ...
>where are your *legs?*"
>"My legs are *gone*

and they won't come back.
My arms are gone
and they won't come back.
My teeth are gone
and they won't come back.
And *you* should have gone home
before it was too late."
The handsome stranger turned and began to twine himself
around the huge tree.
His head disappeared behind that tree,
his body followed after,
and when his head reemerged on the other side of the tree ...
it was the head of a huge ... *snake!*

The handsome stranger ... had changed into a *boa
constrictor!*

Ningun had been following a *snake!*
She turned to run.
But she tripped over the tree's root and fell.
"Aaaaaa" ... the snake-man came slithering out from behind
the tree and began delicately to nibble on her toes!
"Ni ... ni ... ni ... *Ningun* ... ni ... ni ...
Ni ... ni ... ni ... *Ningun* ... ni ... ni ..."
Poor Ningun began to call for help.
*"Ningún-O!
Ningún-O!*
Help oh help Ningún-O!"
Here came a hunter down the road carrying his gun.
It was the very hunter she had turned down.
"Hunter hunter save me!
Hunter save Ningún-O!
Save oh save Ningún-O
This awful awful day!"

The hunter looked.
He saw her toes disappearing into the snake's mouth.
He turned away.

"I don't know Ningún-O,
I don't know Ningún-O,
I won't save Ningún-O
This day or any day."
That snake was swallowing up to her knees.
"Ni ... ni ... ni ... *Ningún* ... ni ... ni
Ni ... ni ... ni ... *Ningún* ... ni ... ni."

"Hunter hunter *save* me!
Hunter save *Ningún-O*
Save oh save Ningún-O
This awful awful day!"
The hunter looked.
Her knees were gone.
He turned away.
"I don't know *Ningún-O,*
I don't know *Ningún-O,*
I won't save *Ningún-O,*
This day or any day."
That boa was swallowing still.
Up to her waist.
"Ni ... ni ... ni ... *Ningún* ... ni ... ni
Ni ... ni ... ni ... *Ningún* ... ni ... ni."
"Hunter hunter *save* me!
Hunter save *Ningún-O*
Save oh save *Ningún-O*
This awful awful day!"

The hunter looked.
The snake had swallowed Ningun clear up to her waist.
He turned away.
"I don't know Ningún-O
I don't know Ningún-O
I won't save Ningún-O
This day or any day."
That snake kept swallowing.
He had reached up to her neck.
"Ni ... ni ... ni ... *Ningún* ... ni ... ni

Ni ... ni ... ni ... *Ningún* ... ni ... ni."
"Hunter hunter *save* me
Save oh save *Ningún-O*
Save oh save *Ningún-O*
This awful awful day."

The hunter looked.
Ningun had disappeared into the snake's body.
Only her pretty little head still stuck out.
He turned away.

      "I don't know *Ningún-O*,
      I don't know *Ningún-O*,
      I won't save *Ningún-O*
      This day or *any* day."

The snake kept swallowing.
      "Ni ... ni ... ni ... *Ningún* ... ni ...
      Ni ... ni ... ni ... *Ningún* ...
The hunter turned.
Already her chin had disappeared into that snake's mouth.
The hunter felt some pity.
He took his gun.
He shot the snake.
The snake writhed.
It died.

Ningun was still in the snake's body.
The hunter took his knife and sliced it open.
He peeled it back and pulled her out.

She was *so* deformed.
From being in that snake's stomach.

      "Oh hunter, you are *so* handsome.
      Now I see that you are *so* handsome.
      Oh hunter, you are *so* strong.
      Now I see that you are *so* strong.

Yes. Yes. I will marry you!"
The hunter looked at her.
    "You? I would as soon marry a goat as marry you.
    You are nothing more than the remains of a snake's
        dinner!"
And he left her there.
So it was with all of the men in that village.
Poor Ningun found no man to marry a *snake's lunch.*

Since that day, no girl in that village may choose her own
    husband.
If a girl wants to marry her father says
    "Fine.
    You
    will marry
    this one!"
And that is that.

Tips for Telling

As the snakeman begins to nibble on Ningun's toes, make the *-gun* of his chant sound like swallowing.

Ni ... ni ... ni ... ningún ... ni ... ni....

Encourage the audience to chant and swallow with you. Experienced audiences can keep up the chant during the entire final portion of the tale, with Ningun's calls and the hunter's retorts playing over the chant. All should be rhythmic.

At the story's end, I point to a specific girl and boy in the audience and deliver the lines. *"You ... will marry ... this one!"* This evokes shrieks of horror from upper elementary and junior high listeners, especially if you size the group up and choose a couple who have been interacting during the stories.

When I tell "Ningun" I always follow it with a simple recounting of the following true story. Such stories can be told in your own words, without much preparation. Their content and their immediacy carry the story without much help on your part.

A True Story: Teresa Olsen, a kindergarten teacher at the Stillwater Elementary School in Carnation, Washington, told me a true story of a man being eaten by a python. It was related to her during a trip with her missionary mother-in-law to a rural Baole village in the Ivory Coast.

It seems this man was a drunkard. He seldom made it back home after his binges and would be found lying asleep along the roadside next morning. One evening when he was lying in the bushes, passed out as usual, a python discovered him.

It started on his right leg. It swallowed and swallowed and swallowed ... until it had swallowed his entire leg. But when it reached his hip it could go no further. The python could not disgorge the entire leg, so it was stuck there.

In the morning the man awoke in a stupor and tried to get up onto his feet. There was a *python* on his leg. He screamed for help and people from the village came to the rescue. They slit the snake and peeled it from his leg. But his leg had been inside the snake all night. The snake's stomach had already begun to *digest* the leg. The skin and the muscles were totally eaten away by the acids of the snake's stomach. The man survived, but he was never able to use that leg again.

The people in this village tell the story to their children to warn them of the dangers of drinking too much. Never drink until you pass out. You never know when a boa will come along and start swallowing *your* leg.

About the Story

"Ningun" is inspired by a version in *One Man, One Wife* by T.M. Aluko (Ibadan: Heinemann, 1967), pp. 20-24. In this novel children are told the story late in the evening as they sit on the veranda. "Toro chanted the solo in her beautiful rich treble voice. All the other children joined in the chorus, clapping their hands to the beats of the music. All except young Dele, who was already dreaming of hunters and boas."

This is Motif B652.1 *Marriage to python in human form.*

Stith Thompson's *Motif-Index of Folk-Literature* cites a Kaffir variant and gives marriage-to-serpent-in-human-form variants from India, Greenland, and the Toba people of South America.

Yonjwa Seeks a Bride

Yonjwa went courting.
Yonjwa was the son of a chief.
Son of Lonkundo, that famous hero.
For such a man a bride must be fine.
No skinny little weaklings for Yonjwa.
A large, strong woman he needed for a wife.

Yonjwa traveled far.
Many villages he passed.
Many women he saw.
But all were too weak … too skinny.
None worthy of a chief's son.

Then one day Yonjwa met a man on the road.
This man was covered with oil,
greasy from top to bottom.
"What on earth happened to *you?*" Yonjwa asked.

> "Oh I did a foolish thing.
> In this next village down the road there is a girl called
>   Eyonga.
> She is the chief's daughter.
> That Eyonga is *so* strong.
> She is large.
> She is handsome.
> She is *beautiful.*
> Everyone wants to marry Eyonga.
> But she won't marry any man.
> When a man comes to court her …
> that Eyonga makes him *wrestle* with her!
> If she can throw him down …
> he has lost.
> But that's not all.
> She makes him wrestle her in a pit of *oil.*

Her father is so rich.
He has palm oil plantations.
That oil is expensive.
But her father fills a pit with palm oil.
And she wrestles standing in that oil.
She rubs that oil all over her body.
She is so slippery.
You can't get a grip on her anywhere.

"I tried to throw her.
Look at me.
She threw me down in that oil.
Everyone laughed.
They ran me out of the village.
It was the most foolish thing I ever tried.
What a fool ... to think I could beat that woman."

When Yonjwa heard this he thought, "At last I may have
found a woman worthy to be my bride!"
Yonjwa went at once to that girl's village.

When he entered he saw a group of girls talking together.
All of them were large, and all of them were beautiful.
But one of those girls was larger and more beautiful than the
others.
She was *gorgeous!*

Yonjwa went right up to her.
"Are you the famous wrestling champion?"
She deigned to look at him.
"I might be."
"Then I have come to *marry* you."
"Oh is that so.
Well, come back tomorrow and we'll *talk* about it."
"No. I have come to marry you ... *today.*"
She looked at him more closely, then turned and walked
away.
"Who *is* this person?"

Yonjwa followed her into the village.
He went right up to the village elders.

>   "Sirs, I have come to marry this woman of yours."
>   "Oh? Well, come back tomorrow, young man, and we
>   will *talk* about it."
>   "No. I have come to marry her *today.*"

"Who *is* this young man?" they asked.
But to Yonjwa they said, "Her *father* isn't here."
Yonjwa was bold. "Then *fetch* him."
They sent for that girl's father and when he came Yonjwa
    spoke.

>   "Sir, I have come to marry your daughter."
>   "Well, come back tomorrow young man.
>   We will *talk* about it."
>   "No. I have come to marry her ... *today.*"
>   "Who *is* this young man?" asked her father.

But to Yonjwa he said. "We have a test here."

>   "Get it ready," said Yonjwa.
>   "I will take the test."

Her father ordered the vat filled with palm oil.
Eyonga jumped into the oil.
She threw palm oil over her shoulders.
She rubbed her face with palm oil.
She was ready.

Yonjwa jumped into the oil.

The oil came up to Eyonga's waist.
The oil came up to Yonjwa's waist.
She was tall.
He was tall.

She was the daughter of a chief.
He was the son of a chief.

She waited.
She watched for her chance.

Eyonga grabbed Yonjwa around the waist.
She lifted him over her head.
> "Aaaaaaannngh!"

She *threw* him into the oil.

Yonjwa jumped up.
Oil was streaming down his face.
He was grinning.
"I *like* this *woman!*"

She grabbed him again.
She lifted him over her head.

> "AAAAAAANGH!"

She *threw* him under the oil.

Yonjwa came up again.
Oil was running from his hair.
He was laughing.
> "I've got to *have* this *woman!*"

She grabbed him again.
This time Yonjwa was ready for her.
Yonjwa got a hold around Eyonga's neck.
He would not let go.
She twisted this way and that.
She tried to throw him and ... both went down beneath the
    oil.

When they came up Yonjwa was still holding on.
He clung to her like a vine to a tree.
Wherever she turned ... there was Yonjwa, hanging fast.
Then ... Yonjwa got his footing.
Slowly ... slowly ... he began to push Eyonga down.
Down ... down ... until she touched the bottom of the vat.
He had *thrown* her!

Those two leapt up.

They were *smiling*.

Eyonga said, "At *last!* A man *strong enough* to be my
    husband!"
Yonjwa said, "At *last!* A woman *strong enough* to be my
    bride!"

Her father said, "Yes. It is a good match.
Tomorrow I will send eight men to bring back the bride price
    from your village."
Yonjwa said
        "Eight *men?*
        You had better send *eighty* men!
        This woman is worth a *lot* of bride price!"
And on the next day Eyonga's father sent eighty men to
    Yonjwa's village.
There Yonjwa filled their baskets so full of bride wealth that
    they could scarcely stagger home.
Such was the price of a good strong woman in *those* days.

Tips for Telling

   I tell this tale boldly, lifting Yonjwa overhead and strain-
ing as I toss him under the oil. He must be very self-confident
and sassy to the elders. The girl is *just* as sassy toward him. I
stress the last line, "Such was the price of a good strong
woman in *those* days."
   Storyteller Debra Harris-Branham created a chant to go
with this tale. She stomps out the rhythm as she chants.

        He looked *here.*
        He looked *there.*
        He couldn't find the right one ...
         any ... where.

   The audience claps and chants with Debra. She interjects
the chant throughout the story and repeats it with the audience as a coda at the story's end. In Debra's hands it is very
effective.

About the Story

This is a small part of the Congolese epic of Lonkundo and his sons. For more of the adventures of Yonjwa and Eyonga see Jan Knappert, *Myths and Legends of the Congo* (Nairobi: Heinemann, 1971). Knappert points out that among the Nkundo, the ideal woman is one of strength and stature.

In the tradition of modern feminism I have altered the tale slightly by omitting Knappert's line, "She knew her master and admired him. He helped her up and she declared herself vanquished." In further episodes Eyonga becomes the mother of the Nkundo people.

The notion of wrestling with one's future bride appears in other cultures, too. Stith Thompson's Motif H331.6.1 *Suitor contest: wrestling with bride* gives Wasco (Native American) and German sources. An Icelandic tale seems related, Motif Q451.0.3 *Strong girl breaks impudent suitor's right hand and left foot.* Aarne and Thompson's *Types of the Folktale* cites Type 519 *The Strong Woman as Bride (Brunhilde)*. Variants are listed from Czechoslovakia, Estonia, Germany, Hungary, Lithuania, Poland, Russia, and Sweden. In this tale, however, the suitor must send a helper to subdue the bride. The ruse is discovered and both the suitor and helper rejected.

Works Cited

Unless they happen to be included in the chapter narratives, this section does not include the items listed in the book's many bibliographies. You will find those indexed by author and title in the index that follows.

Aarne, Antti and Stith Thompson. *The Types of the Folktale*, Folklore Fellows Communications No. 184. Helsinki: Suomalainan Tiedeakatenia, Academia Scientiarum Fennica, 1961.

Adams, Robert J. *Social Identity of a Japanese Storyteller.* Ph.D. Dissertation. Bloomington: Indiana University Press, 1972.

Aluko, T.M. *One Man, One Wife.* Ibadan: Heinemann, 1967.

Anderson, Neil T. and Steve Russo. *The Seduction of Our Children.* Eugene, Oregon: Harvest House, 1991.

Barton, Robert and David Booth. *Writers, Critics, and Children.* New York: Agathon Press, 1976.

Berndt, Catharine. "The Ghost Husband." In *The Anthropologist Looks at Myth*, by Melville Jacobs and John Greenway. Austin: Published for the American Folklore Society by the University of Texas Press, 1966.

Bettelheim, Bruno. *The Uses of Enchantment: The Meaning and Importance of Fairy Tales.* New York: Alfred A. Knopf, Inc., 1976.

Bone, W.A. *Children's Stories and How to Tell Them.* New York: Harcourt, Brace, and Company, 1924.

Borland, Hal. *When the Legends Die.* Philadelphia: J.B. Lippincott, 1963.

Briggs, Katharine M. *A Dictionary of British Folk-Tales.* Bloomington: Indiana University Press, 1970.

Chase, Richard. *Grandfather Tales.* Boston: Houghton Mifflin Co., 1948.

Chatelain, Heli. *Folk-Tales of Angola: Fifty Tales with Ki-Mbundu Text.* Boston and New York: Published for the American Folklore

Society by G.E. Stechert & Co., 1894.

Clarke, Kenneth. *A Motif-Index of the Folktales of Culture-Area V West Africa.* Ann Arbor: University Microfilms International, 1958.

Clarkson, Atelia and Gilbert B. Cross. *World Folktales: A Scribner Resource Collection.* New York: Charles Scribner's Sons, 1980.

Cooper, Pamela J. and Rives Collins. *Look What Happened to Frog: Storytelling in Education.* Scottsdale, Arizona: Gorsuch Scarisbrick Publishers, 1992.

Dayrell, Elphinstone. *Folk Stories From Southern Nigeria.* Westport, Connecticut: Greenwood Publishing Group, 1910. Reprint 1969.

De Vos, Gail. *Storytelling for Young Adults: Techniques and Treasury.* Littleton, Colorado: Libraries Unlimited, 1991.

Degh, Linda. *Folktales and Society.* Bloomington: Indiana University Press, 1969.

Dixon, C. Madeleine. "Once Upon a Time." In *Storytelling*, by the Association for Childhood Education, 1945.

Eastman, Mary Huse. *Index to Fairy Tales, Myths, and Legends.* Westwood, Massachusetts: Faxon, 1926.

_____. *Second Supplement to Index to Fairy Tales, Myths and Legends.* Westwood, Massachusetts: Faxon, 1952.

_____. *Supplement to Index to Fairy Tales, Myths and Legends.* Westwood, Massachusetts: Faxon, 1937.

Finnegan, Ruth. *Limba Stories and Storytelling.* New York: Oxford University Press, 1967.

Galdone, Paul. *The Gingerbread Boy.* New York: Clarion Books, 1975.

Gaster, Theodor H. *The Oldest Stories in the World.* Boston: Beacon Press, 1952.

Godden, Rumer. *Old Woman Who Lived in a Vinegar Bottle.* New York: Viking Press, 1970.

Hearne, Betsy. *The Oryx Multicultural Folktales Series: Beauties and Beasties.* Phoenix: The Oryx Press, 1993.

Hilbert, Vi. *Haboo: Native American Stories from Puget Sound.* Seattle: University of Washington Press, 1985.

Ireland, Norma Olin. *Index to Fairy Tales 1973-1977: Including*

Folklore, Legends, and Myths in Collections. Westwood, Massachusetts: Faxon, 1973.

_____. *Index to Fairy Tales 1949-1972: Including Folklore, Legends, and Myths in Collections.* Westwood, Massachusetts: Faxon, 1973.

Ireland, Norma Olin and Joseph W. Sprug. *Index to Fairy Tales 1978-1986: Including Folklore, Legends, and Myths in Collections.* Metuchen, New Jersey: Scarecrow Press, 1989.

Jacobs, Joseph. *English Folk and Fairy Tales.* New York: The G.P. Putnam's Sons, c. 1898.

Knappert, Jan. *Myths and Legends of the Congo.* Nairobi: Heinemann Books, 1971.

Liestol, Knut and Arthur Garland Jayne. *The Origin of the Icelandic Family Sagas.* Cambridge, Massachusetts: Harvard University Press, 1930.

MacDonald, Margaret Read. *Look Back and See: Twenty Lively Tales for Gentle Tellers.* New York: The H.W. Wilson Co., 1991.

_____. *The Oryx Multicultural Series: Tom Thumb.* Phoenix: The Oryx Press, 1993.

_____. *The Storyteller's Sourcebook: A Subject, Title, and Motif-Index to Folklore Collections for Children.* Detroit: Neal-Schuman/Gale Research, 1982.

_____. *Twenty Tellable Tales: Audience Participation Folktales for the Beginning Storyteller.* New York: The H.W. Wilson Co., 1986.

_____. *When the Lights Go Out: Twenty Scary Tales to Tell.* New York: The H.W. Wilson Co., 1988.

McDermott, Gerald. *Ananse the Spider.* New York: Holt, Rinehart and Winton, 1972.

Michaelsen, Johanna. *Like Lambs to the Slaughter.* Eugene, Oregon: Harvest House, 1989.

Nagishkin, Dmitri. *Folktales of the Amur: Stories from the Russian Far East.* New York: Harry N. Abrams, 1980.

National Directory of Storytelling. Jonesborough, Tennessee: National Association for the Preservation and Perpetuation of Storytelling, annual.

Okeke, Uche. *Tales of Land of Death: Igbo Folktales.* New York: Doubleday, 1971.

P'Bitek, Okot. *Hare and Hornbill.* London: Heinemann Books, 1978.

Pomerantseva, E. *Northern Lights: Fairy Tales of the Peoples of the North.* Translated by Irina Zheleznova. Progress Publishers, 1976.

Postma, Minnie. *Tales From the Basotho.* Austin: University of Texas Press, published for the American Folklore Society, 1974.

Riordan, James. *The Sun Maiden and the Crescent Moon: Siberian Folktales.* New York: Interlink Books, 1989.

Ross, Mabel H. and Barbara K. Walker. *"On Another Day ...":
Tales Told Among the Nkundo of Zaire.* Hamden, Connecticut: Archon Books, 1979.

Sawyer, Ruth. *The Way of the Storyteller.* New York: Viking Press, 1942.

Seitel, Peter. *See So That We May See: Performance and Interpretations of Traditional Tales from Tanzania.* Bloomington: Indiana University Press, 1980.

Seki, Keigo, ed. *Folktales of Japan.* Chicago: University of Chicago Press, 1963.

Shannon, George W.B. *Folk Literature and Children: An Annotated Bibliography of Secondary Materials.* Westport, Connecticut: Greenwood Publishing Group, 1981.

————————. *The Oryx Multicultural Folktale Series: A Knock at the Door.* Phoenix: The Oryx Press, 1992.

Shaw, Spencer G. "First Steps: Storytime with Young Listeners." In *Start Early for an Early Start: You and the Young Child*, edited by Ferne Johnson. Chicago: American Library Association, 1976.

Sierra, Judy. *The Oryx Multicultural Folktale Series: Cinderella.* Phoenix: The Oryx Press, 1992.

Smith, Jimmy Neil. *Homespun: Tales from America's Favorite Storytellers.* New York: Crown Publishing Group, 1988.

Stephens, James. *Crock of Gold.* New York: MacMillan, 1912.

Tedlock, Dennis. *Finding the Center: Narrative Poetry of the Zuni Indians.* Lincoln: University of Nebraska Press, 1972.

Tenenbaum, Joan M. and Mary J. McGary. *Dena'ina Sukdu'a:*

Traditional Stories of the Tanaina Athabaskans. Fairbanks: Alaska Native Language Center, University of Alaska, 1984.

Thompson, Stith. *Motif-Index of Folk-Literature.* Bloomington: Indiana University, 1966.

Thorne-Thomsen, Gudrun. *Storytelling and Stories I Tell.* New York: Viking Press, 1956.

Van der Post, Laurens. *A Walk with a White Bushman.* New York: William Morrow, 1986.

Warren, Jean. "The Pancake Man." In *Totline*, January-February, 1989.

Wolkstein, Diane. *The Magic Orange Tree and Other Haitian Folktales.* New York: Schocken Books, 1980.

Zeitlin, Steven J., Amy J. Kotkin, and Holly Cutting Baker. *A Celebration of American Family Folklore: Tales and Traditions from the Smithsonian Collection.* New York: Pantheon Books, 1982.

Index

This author, title, and subject index will help you locate books on a topic quickly. As the bibliographies are scattered throughout the book, each with its relevant chapter, I think you may find this index useful.

Remember that your local library can obtain these books for you through Interlibrary Loan even if they are not owned by that particular library.